Behold the many and v

Tales of New Al

A deconstructed Steampunk novella in ten short stories.

Conceived and written by Daren Callow

Illuminated and graphitized by Frog Morris

2nd Edition - October 2018

A Monkey Teaspoon Publication, or is it?

ISBN 9781520700304

To understand further the madness herein, please attend:

www.talesofnewalbion.com

Without Whom All This Would Not Be Possible

To all my friends and family that supported me in producing this first humble tome; especially to Carolyn, Emma, Lynda, Maura, Peter/Otis, Vikki, Brian, Tom, Rev Fruitbat and everyone who read or contributed to my early drafts. To all the splendid folk of the Surrey Steampunk Convivials with special mentions to Ben, Catherine, Darren and Steve. To Frog for his wonderful cover art. Last, but on no account least, to my partner, inspiration and muse, thanks Charlie.

Additional thanks to John 'Jags' Smith for kindly proofreading this second edition.

Before Words

I remember very vividly the day that my good friend and esteemed author Mr. Daren Callow wrote to me asking whether I should like to accept his invitation to write a foreword for this book.

Briefly, I felt a little surge of what I presumed might be overwhelming pride (or possibly borborygmus, however I assumed it to be the former) - and recognising that particularly egotistical emotion for the dangerous devil it can become, I humbly reminded myself that forewords are those mostly rambling, oleaginous paragraphs written by people that nobody cares much about, and which no one ever, but ever bothers to read. Full of pithy statements and half-baked sentiment. How I detest them. [1]

What I find particularly irritating is that they always seem to have a spurious or indecipherable quote in Latin (which few, if any of us studied, or retained), always in italics to give them a sense of superiority;

Parturient montes, nascetur ridicus mus.

In any event, I suppose whilst prefaces in themselves do not detract overmuch from the book as a whole, the inclusion of a preface must embody what I can only assume to be a somewhat thinly veiled attempt to fill up those blank pages, which would otherwise nestle undisturbed somewhere between the table of contents and the introduction.

And what a waste those dry pages are! Why, books have been made since the very dawn of literature, and always with one or two blank pages at the beginning and end. And to what end?

If mankind had saved up all of those utterly unused and unsullied pieces of paper that have queued up silently at either end of every book we have ever read, I feel sure that at least one horde of monkeys might have been closer to finishing The Complete Works of Shakespeare. Better still, if it were possible to abandon the idea of a foreword, and do away with the virgin pages altogether, there would be more trees on the planet. How I love trees! [2]

After mulling this over for a few weeks, I decided the only course of action would be to politely decline Mr. Callow's invitation based on the logic that by not including pages for a foreword, there could be more trees in the world and he'd then have to agree that would be a good thing.

However, for fear of offending my dear friend I must here and now humiliate myself and admit that I procrastinated terribly, and put off telling him that I planned to turn down his offer. To be honest, I'd put any thought of being involved completely behind me. It was, as it were out of sight, out of mind.

However, seven years later whilst on a mountaineering expedition, the strangest coincidence occurred. My party was just over halfway up the west flank of the Eiger, as I recall, overlooking Grindelwald in the Burmese Alps of Switzerland.

I happened to bump into a former groundsman of Mr. Callow, who was on his way down. Good man, no idea why he was let go. Went by the name of Mr. Clonderalaw.

Now, he told me that the book had in fact been ready for publication for years, and that my good friend the respectable author Mr. Callow had delayed putting it into print for all this time because he was patiently waiting for me to respond to his request to write a foreword for it.

Needless to say, I felt suitably awkward and chagrined, and on my return to Ol' Blighty, I resolved to get in touch with my dear old friend Mr. Callow and beg his forgiveness, write that blasted foreword, and get his book into print.

But I am ashamed to admit that once again, foolish pride and embarrassment prevented me. I was crippled with shame, which made me as timid as a mouse.

So, instead I wrote this. And my betting is, he'll never read it anyway, and neither will you.

Anyway, Daren's a thoroughly good egg, and here follows his book. I'm sure you'll enjoy it. His last edition of this book was amazing, I have to say: one of my favourite editions, and it never had a foreword. Probably. Well, if it did, I didn't notice.

Ben Henderson, somewhere in Surrey.

[1] Especially those with footnotes.

[2] Apart from silver birch.

What Layeth Herewithin

I

Timeshock

Little could they have known, as our protagonists were collected two by two in Sir Grenville Lushthorpe's belching steam coach, the sheer scale of the imminent disaster they were about to inflict upon an unsuspecting city.

First to be embarked were Philby the callow be-suited journalist and Ellen Hall the fearless explorer ravishing in leather jacket and khaki jodhpurs.

'Some wheeze eh?' she remarked leaping aboard, Philby did not reply, as he brushed his hair shyly from his eyes and climbed in after her, notebook and pencil clamped in sweaty hands. The charabanc lurched on; the city's streets were dimly lit by flickering gas lamps made more eerie by an early evening mist settling in every gutter and back alley.

Onwards, onwards to Bankside, where the river was at full swell, foaming angrily at the sides of the embankment. Here they halted again to collect First Lord of the Admiralty Cuthbert and his good lady wife Eliza, in high spirits following a belly-filling luncheon at the Conway Club.

'Well, well, well,' he muttered, doffing his hat to Ellen as he squeezed his well-proportioned frame through the ornate door of the coach. He nodded, without really looking, at Philby and promptly sat himself in the front-most seat. 'A right escapade and no mistake.' Eliza was barely seated before the coach jerked on its way to collect the final witnesses of that fateful night.

Eyebrows were raised amongst the motley crew as the final rendezvous turned out to be no less than the 'Minster itself, as the PM, no less, and his Special Branch man (scandalously the PM was not married) stood impatiently under the nominated lamppost.

'What nonsense do you think Lushthorpe has planned up for us tonight, eh?' muttered the PM to no one in particular as each acknowledged the other and the final leg of their night's adventure began. By this time the mists were gathering into a white blanket of fog, but the coach had a good many modern lights and the pilot knew his business. Thankfully for the backsides of all in the jalopy the clanking, steaming drive to Sir Lushthorpe's east end laboratory was made in good time and Cuthbert snored only the once.

Lushthorpe's city dwelling was a deceptively impressive establishment. The front itself looked like many of the smart townhouses alongside in its quiet cul-de-sac. However once ushered over the threshold by a pair of butlers (one male, one female) in natty tails the full extent of the property began to reveal itself. A large hallway, with sweeping staircases to the upper floors, was harder to navigate than should have been the case due to the large number of eccentric contraptions positioned all around. Chief amongst these were a gas-powered voice-o-graph and another device that looked to all the world like a four-horned gramophone mounted on a carousel mechanism rotating laconically in a giant fish tank, an occasional bubble of air drifting to the surface. Here the bubbles would pop and emit a strangled musical note, although it was hard to discern any obvious tune. There was no time for the guests to consider its possible use before Lushthorpe himself entered grandly from a previously concealed side door.

'You are here, you are here, wonderful,' he greeted them, waving his thin arms wildly, 'It is no word of a lie, dare I say it, that what I will show you tonight will change your lives forever!' Little did they know it, but never had more truthful words been spoken.

Lushthorpe himself was an odd man of lean build, but with a slight hunch to his gait. He was attired in waistcoat and breeches of his own singular design, his hair was scraggy, thinning and grey, but his eyes were alight with the wonders he was impatient to reveal. Around his neck were a pair of silvered goggles and a baroque watch and chain completed the eccentric look. 'You must forgive my lack of introductions, there are a great many elemental wheels in motion tonight, some of which are so unstable that we may only have a slim window to observe their wonders.' More hand waving accompanied this speech, his clockwork cuff links glinting tantalisingly in the orange gaslight. 'Follow me with all haste to the scene of the crime.' With this choice of words the Special Branch man frowned for an instance, but the PM waved him aside and boldly led the gang after the scientist as he strode across the hall and through the baroque double-doors at the far side.

Lushthorpe moved with quite a lop through three more sets of equally elegant doors and down corridors that often turned through sharp bends. Lady Eliza was forced to gather her skirts in order to keep pace with them all. Finally when the First Lord was all but ready to ask for a time out they breached the final threshold and entered what appeared to be a medium-sized ballroom to see

Lushthorpe's wife making the final adjustments to what seemed to be quite a modest pair of contraptions in the very middle of the room.

'Golly *is* that it?' Ellen was heard to mutter under her breath.

The first of the puzzling devices took the form of a particularly well appointed camera with four bronze ringed lenses of varying sizes, mounted on and connected directly to, a large copper ducting tube which plunged vertically into the hardwood floor. A myriad of lesser pipework accompanied the larger on its journey downwards, some appeared to be frosted with ice, whereas others could be glimpsed glowing red hot beneath their insulating sleeves. It was in front of this peculiar apparatus that Lushthorpe now ushered all those in the room. Lushthorpe's wife, a robust and earnest looking woman of eastern continental appearance who went by the name of Griselda, stood behind a control panel formed of several dials, large switches and electrical circuit breakers and four score vacuum tubes mounted in a shelved arrangement, all aglow in a kaleidoscope of light. Mrs Lushthorpe did not look up and said nothing, as was her way.

'If you could please stand within the focal area of the timescope I would be most obliged.' He glanced at his wife, who gave barely a glimmer of a raised eyebrow in response. 'Ah yes, it seems I have a little time to explain your mysterious summoning tonight.' The attendees raised a few eyebrows of their own as they cautiously stepped before the barrels of the device. 'Fear not, fear not there is nothing to be afraid of,' reassured the inventor. 'Do not concern yourself with keeping still either, it is vital for my demonstration tonight that you act normally and er, very much, be yourselves, as it were.'

'It's not a death ray then Lushy old boy?' heckled the First Lord jovially, which caused the Special Branch man to look nervous again.

'I think perhaps he intends to suck out our souls,' interjected Ellen slyly. The First Lord slapped his thigh at this and guffawed with laughter so much that the PM was forced to give him a stern look. 'By the way, where is that lad of yours? Or is this all too dangerous for a minor to be in attendance?'

'The timescope is perfectly safe,' snapped Lushthorpe, 'unstable perhaps, but safe nonetheless.' He glanced around him to ascertain firstly the machine was still functioning correctly, and secondly that his boy had not sneaked unseen into the room. 'Tom has been in one of his moods today, I have not seen him since breakfast.'

'A shame,' the First Lord replied, 'the lad is quite the prankster, I'm sure he would have enlivened things'.

'Trust me, no *enlivening* will be required. What you are about to witness is quite conceivably the most incredible experience since the dawn of time itself.'

'Quite a boast Lushthorpe,' interjected the PM placing his thumbs in his waistband, 'I'm all ears to hear what you have created.' Lushthorpe did not seem to hear him as he was really beginning to warm to his theme.

'Beneath this very building is a mile-long circular tunnel which is connected by electro-magnet lined pipework to this very instrument you see before you.' He tapped his hand vigorously on the camera contraption, which caused his Griselda to look at him wide-eyed. The PM considered enquiring if he had obtained the necessary planning permissions, but thought better of it in the end as Lushthorpe barely paused for breath. 'Through this tunnel I have devised a method to accelerate particles to such speeds that I am able to move them backwards and, indeed, forwards through the fabric of time itself.'

This revelation was greeted by a sharp intake of breath and a second later all in the room, bar Griselda, jumped in unison as an unheralded sharp burst of steam erupted through one of the pipes to startling effect.

'Now look here Lushthorpe,' opened the PM, 'are you telling us that you have invented a time machine?' he continued.

'Of sorts, of sorts; in point of fact the timescope is merely a passive conduit to the manifold dimensions of time that surround us all. In due course I do intend to master travel in these spheres, but for now this will have to suffice.'

'But what the dickens is the blasted thing?' The First Lord snapped with growing impatience. His mood was not enhanced by a second burst of steam through an entirely different outlet, they all jumped again. When he had regained his composure Lushthorpe glanced again at his wife, and seemingly assured by some unseen signal he turned back to those present. 'Well now, I do believe it's finally time for you to see for yourselves.'

Without further words Griselda relinquished her place at the controls and Lushthorpe indicated that they should move to stand behind the second of the two installations in the room. This gleaming device positioned four yards or so behind the camera apparatus, consisted of a matching large pipe this time rising up from the floor in a similar fashion. The pipe fed into a square metal box with a similar contingent of accompanying ancillary pipes, wires and even some softly ticking clockwork mechanisms. On each of the four horizontal panels of the box was mounted a polished brass viewfinder, that looked to all the world like the eyepieces of a saucy end-of-the-pier mutoscope.

'Are we about to see what the butler saw?' smirked Ellen to Philby who was so dazed he had yet to make a single note in his now slightly crumbled pad.

'Not only will you see *what* the butler saw, you will see what she *will* see also,' smirked Lushthorpe cryptically. 'For this is the viewing box of my timescope, by looking through the apertures whilst I manipulate these controls,' he gestured flamboyantly towards the control box, 'you will be able to witness, with your own mortal eyes, every event to have occurred in the arc of the assimilator for several hundred years in the past!' Another collective intake of breath, 'moreover,' he spat through slightly foaming lips, 'I am able to show you, this very night, every event to occur in the same vicinity for several hundred years into the future!'

'Good lord Lushy!' burbled the First Lord animatedly, 'Are you saying you can see into the future with this devilish contraption?'

'I am, and what is more, I will show you here and now.'

An overexcited babble arose as Griselda approached proffering goggles with slotted grills across them and each attendee took a pair.

'Now this I have to see,' ventured Ellen already angling to take one of the eyepieces.

'Ladies first of course,' gestured the PM to Ellen and Eliza whilst simultaneously making it clear with his body language that no one should be mistaken that he was next in line for a berth.

'Goggles on please,' spoke up Griselda for the first time in her sharp Germanic accent which, amusingly had there been any additional observers in the room, caused all to look at her with surprise on their faces.

'Indeed all should put on the goggles now including the attendants.' With this Lushthorpe gestured towards Philby and the policeman who had already realised they were not in line for the initial viewing. Padded leather stools had been provided and once suitably begoggled Eliza, Ellen, The First Lord and the PM made themselves comfortable around the four viewfinders. Philby, finally finding some gumption, had begun scribbling in his pad. The Special Branch man shuffled from foot to foot and continued to glance around in a nervous fashion.

'I say Lushthorpe, it's awfully hard to see through these goggles,' griped the PM fiddling with the eyepieces.

'Regrettably you must wear the goggles to protect yourselves from stray accelerated particles. You may also experience some blurring of the image, but remember this is the cutting edge of today's technology and you are my pioneers. Please make yourselves comfortable on the apparatus whilst I explain what you are about to see.'

With much nervous anticipation the two ladies and gentlemen leant forward and positioned their eyes against the brass eyepieces.

At first it was hard to make much out, but as Lushthorpe and Griselda manipulated both the control levers and a second bank of complicated machinery at the far side of the ballroom, a blurred view of the wall they had just been standing in front of slowly came into focus. More steam vented noisily into the room and beneath their feet the floor vibrated slightly and then more firmly before this rattling motion faded away. The lights in the room also dimmed as Lushthorpe announced dramatically, 'And Lo! Behold! THE PRESENT!'

Indeed it seemed a fair declaration that they were indeed viewing the wall in real time, a sense of disappointment was palpable.

'I can view the present without this blasted contraption,' muttered the First Lord his impatience returning.

'You will recall,' continued Lushthorpe with undimmed enthusiasm, 'that on entering this room I asked you to stand in this very line of sight. I will now manipulate the machinery beneath our feet to enable us to see ourselves *in the past.*' He bent over the dials again and this time manipulated a large brass wheel, the floor began to vibrate again, but this time it did not diminish as before. As this happened the lights dimmed further and slowly, blurred figures began to appear in the viewfinders.

'I see them,' chirped Eliza excitedly, and sure enough the blobs now came into focus and the figures were revealed to be the six of them standing nervously as they had been early directed.

'I see us too,' added Ellen, 'we are really seeing the past.'

'Lushy you bloody devil!' bellowed the First Lord quite flabbergasted 'There I am, all bloomin' twenty stone of me!'

The PM, however, said nothing as a cold shiver ran down his spine; he could barely believe what he was witnessing. But sure enough the whole scene played out in eerie, jerky motion. He watched spellbound as his own ghostly figure tucked its thumbs into its waistband. Then a spontaneous burst of laughter from all four as they saw themselves jump in fright at the first burst of steam.

'But this is the mere beginning! Behold as I reverse time still further!' By now all the viewers were so rapt that no more comprehensible words passed their lips as, with fiendish skill, Lushthorpe manipulated the controls of his device to show them further and further back in time. First the decoration on the wall changed to an older style. Shadowy figures moved in and out of focus as steam emissions and vibrations caused the room and the mechanism to throb around them. The visible figures seemed so tantalising, very real yet achingly fleeting; as these avatars from the past had no knowledge that more advanced eyes from the future were observing them and, frustratingly, they rarely made any effort to stay in the field of vision.

There was yet another gasp from the four of them when the wall suddenly disappeared and visible instead was a trampled earthen lane and a low rustic mediaeval dwelling. This in turn gave way to rolling fields, then to wooded land. All through this the picture glowed and then dimmed as night followed day, winter followed summer and streams of clouds and the years flicked past in their line of sight like some epic motion picture run backwards. It was a full half hour before the picture finally faded to black and they all jumped in their seats yet again as Griselda barked, 'Step away from the eyepieces!' It seemed the magnificent contraption had run out of power for the time being and the participants reluctantly peeled themselves away and removed their goggles. Over the commotion and excitement of the spectacle none of them had heard the twin butlers enter and set up chairs and a table resplendently laid out with chilled wine and a rather delicious looking supper. The four initial witnesses retired gratefully to this feast their mouths a jabber with the scarcely believable experience they were struggling to comprehend. Lushthorpe meanwhile reset the machine and graciously ran the entire sequence again, this time with rather less hyperbole, to permit Philby and the Special Branch man to also serve witness to history in the making.

At The First Lord's insistent bidding the butlers two were despatched to find the lad -Tom - to also attend the proceedings, but alas no trace of him could be found.

Once all present had viewed their fill of the past and filled their bellies with sufficient cold meat and cheese, glasses were raised in a toast to what was unanimously declared to be the invention of the age. Once this formality was complete Lushthorpe cleared his throat and rose to speak. In solemn tones that caused all the guests to pay full attention he began:

'As you have all borne witness, I have created here, by my own devising a machine capable of viewing varied times through history.' Nods of agreement all around were interrupted as the First Lord took a loud draft of wine from his fluted glass, which did not go down so well with the others.

'We have viewed, with alacrity, a plethora of visages of the recent and indeed, somewhat less recent past. These scenes we may view with impunity and untroubled countenance, since they are gone and done with and no person may be affected by what we witness except, naturally, to increase their understanding of our ancestors and the world within which they dwelt.' He paused dramatically for effect, 'the same cannot be said of the future!

'As the first of our species to be able to witness events not only from the past, but from the time yet to come, it is incumbent on us not to view anything that might prove compromising to those present amongst us. Indeed, it is my solemn recommendation that rather than viewing the immediate future, we should look instead to view events long after we have shuffled off this mortal coil.'

The PM in particular seemed deep in thought at this suggestion, and he was first to offer an additional opinion, 'I am inclined to agree with you. It would be a tragedy of great proportion for any of us to witness, however fleetingly, some harrowing event in one of our lives. Or, indeed, something that enabled us to take advantage over others with the knowledge of what is yet to come.' It was the PM's turn to pause for effect, 'I would concur that perhaps a visage of the world two or three hundred years hence should satisfy our desire for knowledge without compromising anyone's position in the world.' There were nods around the table at this proposal, which Lushthorpe took to denote tacit approval.

'Very well, it is my earnest belief that following my previous experiments and with the experience of tonight's practical demonstration under my belt, I am now able to manipulate the timescope with exceptional accuracy to any date in the past or future that is within its range.' He stood, replaced his goggles and indicated that the others should do likewise. 'Re-attend the machine now and I will show you a vision two hundred years, give or take, in the future of our very lives. No soul living nor dead has witnessed such a thing before us!' And with this dramatic pronouncement ringing in their ears, they all rose and made their way back to their positions around the device.

No talk was necessary now as all knew the drill, Philby scribbled feverishly in his pad and the Special Branch man looked on trepidatiously as the other four took their seats. Lushthorpe reset his controls and made sure they knew not to attend the viewfinders until he was confident they were viewing sufficiently distant into the future.

Once again the floor vibrated, wires hummed and steam vented in a manner that seemed even more portentous, were such a thing possible in a machine.

'We are approaching the time, prepare yourselves for a meeting with destiny,' uttered Lushthorpe, a slight nervous croak in his voice clearly audible. The vibrations in the floor were now exceeding anything experienced previously, and without warning a strong smell of ammonia filled the room.

'DO NOT BE ALARMED!' shouted Griselda in an extremely alarming manner. The lights dimmed again and an eerie glow filled the room as the valves in the machine glowed ominously. Lushthorpe dared not take his eyes from the controls, but as the moment approached he raised an arm with one finger pointing to the group.

'Nearly!' All looked nervously around them, adjusting goggles once more and making sure they were well seated so as to not embarrass themselves with a slip when the future was revealed. Each attendee's minds began to fill with possibilities, just what would the future hold for this fragile planet of theirs?

'It is time! Behold the very world we inhabit, two hundred years hence!'

The four witnesses bent quickly to their viewfinders and let their eyes adjust to the vision before them.

'Well that's rum,' remarked the First Lord after a short time had passed.

'What vision attends you?' gibbered Lushthorpe feverishly.

'Well not a lot really, I can just see the wall. What about the rest of you?' Murmurs to the affirmative indicated that all were seeing the same thing, a glowing, flickering, but very clearly visible view of the very same wall as was before them now. Lushthorpe moved to the viewfinders and, rather uncouthly, pushed the PM to one side so he could take a look.

'Well I'll be, you are quite right.' Without even removing his goggles Lushthorpe slid a slide rule from his pocket and made some on-the-hoof calculations that he crosschecked against the positions and read-outs of the various levers and dials.

'It all seems correct, I don't really understand. What has befallen this house that nothing has happened to it in two centuries?'

'Are you sure the blinking thing is working, why would the room be abandoned and not attended for so long?' inquired the PM, somewhat annoyed that he had been pushed aside so casually.

'Fear not, I will go forward in time to the limit of the machine, another hundred years should be possible, attend your positions.' The PM and all concerned leaned in once more as a similar routine of rumblings took place.

'Behold the future three hundred years distant!' Lushthorpe's announcement was well intoned, but regrettably the vision in the viewfinders remained stubbornly and frustratingly the same – a blank, unaltered wall.

Much discussion now broke out amongst the ensemble as Philby, Special Branch, Griselda and Lushthorpe all took turns at the viewers, but no discernable change in the vista could be detected. Amidst much checking and re-checking of the still rumbling machine, it was suggested that perhaps the building was abandoned or preserved for some reason. Maybe connected with the historic events of this very soiree. Only the PM's voice seemed to have a concern that more ominous events might have caused the abandonment, and in the end it was he who suggested, nay demanded, further manipulation of the machine to make sure.

'It concerns me greatly that we might be witnessing an abandonment of the building for several hundred years hence. Is it possible that by playing with the unseemly forces of nature tonight we have unleashed some malevolent force on the world?' This suggestion did not go down well.

'Poppycock,' offered Lushthorpe with hopes of dashing all doubt, but others were also starting to fret.

One more attempt to view the furthest date in the future possible by the device was attempted. By Lushthorpe's increasingly feverish calculations they were looking nearly five hundred years into the future. The vision was faint, but unsettling all the same. The wall had obviously decayed somewhat in the intervening period, but it appeared as if no human hand had touched it in all that time. It was hard to say for certain, but someone claimed to have seen a rat, and also plants could be seen growing in a crack to the left of the image.

In the end it was Ellen's younger and sharper eyesight that spotted a possible clue in the very bottom right corner of the dim, flickering image.

'It looks like a pile of small bones!' she exclaimed, causing all to hurriedly return to look and there was a slight jostle as it soon became clear that eight into four was not going to go. Lushthorpe, the PM, The First Lord and, obviously, Ellen the initial finder ended up in the pole positions.

'By Jove, she's bally right,' proffered the First Lord, 'Bones it is, how did we not notice before?' Similar views were offered by all and a hurried, and with hindsight somewhat hasty, decision was made to reverse the machine and try to identify the poor unfortunate creature that had been the original bone donor, so to speak.

'Oh my, I do hope it's not a person,' squeaked Philby. All seconded his views and a very distinct chill descended on the room despite the manic rumblings of the timescope contraption all around them.

Back they went in time, year followed year, until there could be no debate on the unfortunate object. It was hard to see through the combination of goggles and flickering viewfinder, but clearly visible in the bottom of the picture was the ghostly white foot of a human skeleton!

By this point the First Lord and Eliza had lost their stomach for viewing the grisly scene and retired, pale-faced, to down more wine. Special Branch and Philby were suddenly in their element and along with the PM and Ellen resolved that a decision was needed. Special Branch, whose name turned out to be Quentin, took charge of the situation as Lushthorpe was observed to be shaking slightly and the PM seemed utterly lost for words.

'It seems that our very worst fears have been realised.' He paced backwards and forwards, if he had had a pipe to hand, no doubt he would have sucked on it thoughtfully. 'Exactly as Lushthorpe cautioned us, we are all now witness to an unfortunate event. The facts as I see them are as follows; at some point in the future, through accident, design or foul malevolent force of nature a poor soul has lost its life in this very room.' At this statement, Griselda gave an alarming wail and left the room noisily to resume a frantic search for her son.

'I knew it,' muttered the PM, finally rediscovering his vocabulary, 'by your unnatural workings you have unleashed some violent force upon the earth!' He was beginning to shake now. 'This should never have taken place, we should never come here, we have gone against god and now we will all pay!'

'Easy now,' interrupted Ellen trying to keep her voice level, although her anxiety was growing too. 'We don't know that for sure.'

'We don't indeed,' it was Quentin who stepped in now. 'But by the power invested in me, I demand that we reverse the machine still further and view what took place.'

'Even if we glimpse something unnatural?' blurted the PM.

'Even so.'

Grimly, amidst some sobbing, the decision was made to do as had been suggested. For better or worse, Lushthorpe had no choice but to comply.

In silence the four, by now pale-faced, witnesses – Ellen, Quentin, Philby and the PM returned to their duty. The First Lord and his wife continued to drink, but made no other noises as the machine was reversed and time was rolled back. No one noticed the noise and vibrations as they were each fixed on their task.

Slowly the years peeled back again and the grisly bones grew flesh, first decayed and putrid, held by strips of material, then more formed and complete. Ellen put a hand to her mouth as a monstrous rat was clearly seen in the peculiar act of *replacing* a shoe onto the foot. Philby lurched alarmingly on his stool and then hurried to a corner and was sick. Everyone began to feel nauseous as the vile smell joined the others in the room. Lushthorpe was seemingly unmoved, rolling his machine backwards in time inexorably towards the present. The foot, now dressed and shod, was clear for all to see, lying prone on the floor of the room – a man's foot or perhaps since there was nothing to reference the size against, horror of horrors, a boy's.

Back and back the machine took them until, without warning the leg simply disappeared.

'Good god,' muttered Quentin, 'well I never.' At this comment the First Lord returned to the vacated viewer and the unrelenting near future image of the wall only a few feet away from them, nothing else now being visible.

'We are almost back at the present' whispered Lushthorpe, unsure whether anyone was listening to him anymore.

It was at this point, with the Prime Minister of the land and the First Lord of the Admiralty as witnesses alongside a much respected member of the senior constabulary and a renown explorer, that the most horrific, blood-curdling sight that you might ever imagine from now until your dying day appeared in the view finder of the infernal machine. Briefly, with heart-stopping suddenness and with no prior hint it was about to happen a ghastly face that appeared to be the devil himself appeared in the viewfinder. Blood red eyes, gnarled horns, snarling teeth, bleeding red tears and looking directly at them! The PM fainted on the spot and collapsed to the floor. Quentin and Ellen fought to prevent themselves being sick whilst the First Lord let out a blood-curdling scream not entirely dissimilar to a cat being strangled. Lushthorpe, who thankfully had not witnessed the awful visage, lost his footing at the shock of it all and fell into the control box damaging it and plunging the room briefly into darkness as the machine ground to a halt and the viewfinders faded to black.

With practiced speed the butlers appeared with hurricane lamps and evacuated the ensemble out of the dreaded room. The PM was roused and he immediately ordered the evacuation of the city lest the evil apparition killed more people.

With growing anxiety and desperation Lushthorpe and his wife searched further for their beloved Tom, but with no trace found they resigned themselves that the evil force had made him the first victim. As the sirens wailed across the city and with aching hearts they left with the others and joined the stream of bewildered refuges away from epicentre of doom.

None of them would ever return to this cursed house.

After nearly half an hour of silence in the creaking and mostly darkened house, the boy Tom decided to crawl out of his wonderful new hiding place. Without a word, lest he fail to successfully sneak up on any unsuspecting adults, he made his way out from under the stairs and across to the doors of the medium-sized old ballroom where his mother and father abandoned him daily to work. He leant against the door straining his ears to hear if there was anyone within. He heard nothing, so tentatively tried the door and then opened it to find the room empty apart from the hastily abandoned supper and the still creaking and steaming remains of the now terminally damaged timescope. Walking carefully across the room towards the assimilator he reached into his waistband and pulled out the Hallowe'en mask he had intended to don to scare his parents, and for want of something more interesting to do, he put it on anyway. It had a realistic devilish appearance that he had designed and lovely crafted in solitary moments over the last couple of weeks. Mask in place he trod carefully in his slightly too big school shoes across the floor to what appeared to be a four-lensed camera and peered into it, wondering what its use might be. It held little interest for him, and appeared to do nothing at all, so mask still affixed he wandered off into the house to see just where everyone had gone.

II

Tobias Fitch

The imposing bulk of Tobias Fitch filled the doorway of the very last coach of the TTCE as it puffed, wheezed and clanked to a halt at Fin Du Monde station. He hesitated for just a heartbeat or two scanning the almost deserted platform, allowing his senses to read any signs of danger before his body was even fully awake. It had been a long and restless journey, but at least it hadn't been the route that had caused him a sleepless night. The TTCE (Tri Transcontinental Express) was a brutally simple idea; three parallel tracks with three state-of-the-art rocket assisted Sky Legend class locomotives harnessed together like a modernist's team of horses. Between them they pull a single line of armoured sleeper cars, the power to weight ratio ensuring seemingly effortless acceleration. The only drawback being that bends are not exactly on the cards for this particular three-headed iron dragon. So the TTCE line (the only one there is) ploughs a relentlessly straight triple furrow from one side of the continent to the other, equally disdainful of border, personal property or natural obstacle. Pretty much how Fitch himself liked to operate. His only regret on this cold, grey, blustery morning was that the triple-tracked train couldn't deliver him and his precious cargo directly into the bustling heart of the old metropolis.

Gratified that platform 13 seemed to hold no immediate threats to his aching body, Fitch wrapped his floor-length leather trenchcoat around him, and put a booted foot firmly onto the narrow brick strip. In his left hand he held a battered, but extremely robust looking attaché case, his grip was firm and he held it close whilst still viewing the vicinity with caution. The tight hold however, was somewhat superfluous as the case in question was in fact fastened to his wrist by means of a heavy chain and brass handcuff. So precious, so vital to national security were its contents that he could not allow himself to be separated from it under any circumstances: casual, accidental or violent. His right hand hovered constantly in the opening of his coat near his hips, where a brace of custom-made, silver-plated pistols hung in quick draw holsters. The seven-chambered weapons had extricated him from trouble on numerous occasions when opponents had reckoned on only six bullets per loading. The thick leather of his coat hid other secrets too, additional weapons; including assorted throwing knives, grenades, poisons and a smaller automatic pistol; plus steel plating over vital organs and arteries. All of this now conspired with his aching, sleep-deprived limbs, to make the walk from the back of the train to the front of the monster all the more laboured. Nevertheless Fitch did not regret the slow progress; it gave him time to go meticulously over the final details of his four-day long journey. Fitch had been tasked, by rocket-assisted pigeon, at barely an hour's notice, to retrieve the case from a numbered locker at a far-flung empire postal depot, secure it to his person and then make his way by airship, steam-powered paddle steamer and stage coach to the furthest terminus of the TCCE. He had then carefully selected the very last sleeper cabin in the train for its two-day cross-continental rush. The final leg of this clandestine adventure was to cross the channel and deliver his cargo to another anonymous safe locker at Kings Station, where, he was assured the release key and his six figure pay-off awaited him in return. There were only three methods by which this crossing could be effected from here, a slow and cheap steamer, a more expensive but a little quicker, airship service or, and the selection of this means hinted again at the importance of his mission, an extremely expensive, but very fast, personal ornithopter flight. According to terse instructions, the crossing was booked and the pilot was waiting at a nearby aerodrome, Fitch need make no other arrangements bar finding a taxi cab to transport him there.

Coming up to the business end of the locomotives the noise and general hubbub of the platform swelled in intensity. Here the three engines were being slowly uncoupled, on their parallel tracks, by a small number of grimy engineers seemingly from all corners of the globe. The outside trains were used in transit to pull a sizable number of coal tenders and the system of pulleys and conveyor belts used to feed the boilers, each tender being discarded as they emptied to increase speed still further. Anxious to locate the cab rank and not tarry too long in an unknown location Fitch continued his clumping stride into the maelstrom of metal, bustling workers and hissing steam, peering forward to try and locate a porter or other station worker to guide him. Through the fog he spied a man in smart blue uniform, peaked cap and elegant (if somewhat exotic) curled black moustache that seemed to fit the bill. Raising his free hand he attempted to hail him, but lost him briefly in another snort of steam from the engines. Clearing the vapour he expected to see the man only a yard or so away from him, but to his annoyance, and no little surprise, there was no sign of the porter. Indeed the forecourt of the station seemed entirely deserted of both staff and passengers. He spun on his heels trying to locate the official, but could see no glimpse of anyone of his appearance within a hundred yards, indeed right up to the station arches. It was as if the man had, to all intents and purposes, simply vanished into thin air. This disturbed Fitch somewhat, he liked certainty and solidity in his world and this did not fit at all. He rubbed his eyes and tried to put aside the nagging doubt that this curious apparition had some connection to his top-secret cargo, preferring instead to put it down to tiredness and a trick of the dawn light. He reached into his great coat and extracted a small, but ornately carved pill case. Popping it open he selecting something to liven his senses and swallowed it swiftly. With a tired shrug he swung his night bag further onto his shoulder and strode on towards the station portico where, he reasoned, a suitably less ephemeral taxi might be hailed.

Outside the station the world was beginning to wake up from it's drowsy slumber. The light was on the gloomy side of dull and the wind brisk as Fitch made a cautious approach to the meagre taxi rank. A mere three conveyances were making themselves available for service this early in the morning. Two were horse-drawn and the third, a particularly unkempt looking iron wagon seemingly powered by a multi-patched gas bag that caught every gust of wind and appeared inclined to blow away at any second. One of the horses seemed the much safer bet, even though as he approached one of the cabs the harnessed nag appeared to be somewhat troubled by his presence. The cabbie seemed less bothered and attempted to calm the beast and smarten himself a little in the hope of a good tip early in the day. The driver was dark skinned and heavy featured, a well-used leather jerkin spoke of many years hard work, but he was presentable enough. He tugged down a chainmail face guard to reveal an uneven mouth.

'Where to sir?' Fitch was impressed that the man had realised he was not local and spoken in English, but rather less impressed when he added 'Wind's up a bit.' He had no time to discuss the weather and with a surly 'Aerodrome Rothschild' he hauled himself and his two bags into the cabin and slammed the wooden panelled door shut. If the driver was offended he gave no sign of it, taking up the horse's leather reins he hauled himself up onto the driver's seat, re-adjusted his metal face covering and bade the horse be off which, with only a little reluctance, it obeyed.

The interior of the cab was dark and musty, with a crude metal speaking tube for communicating with the pilot; Fitch had no time for this either and banged the cover shut. The doors had only small metal slits with no glass, which meant that the passenger was somewhat exposed to the elements even within. Fitch did not mind this as it meant he was reasonably well protected from prying eyes. Nevertheless he stowed his case and bag carefully alongside on the upholstered seat and then eased one of his silver pistols out onto his lap to facilitate its instantaneous use should the need arise. The strange incident in the steam had unsettled him and the upper he had taken served now to only increase his sense of agitation. Although he had been told nothing officially about the nature of the case and its contents a man of Fitch's profession tended to not survive very long without having a keen sense what he was being asked to get involved in. The original location of the case, the vast amount of money being thrown at its return by fast, but highly unorthodox routes, pointed him in one direction only: the Fourth Day Ascension League, a highly illegal underground society whispered to be advocates of black magic and even necromancy. Rumoured to have origins in the darkest areas of the sub-continent the league's tentacle-like fingers were believed to have crept into the very highest echelons of power across the continent and even into the homeland itself. Not wanting to speculate too much, as it was not his way, Fitch could only assume that the items contained within the chained case were critical in some way to beating this deadly and mysterious cult. He could only hope.

Glancing out the narrow slit in the door, it was clear they were leaving the outskirts of the town and heading towards an expanse of open countryside that was likely to be the aerodrome. Another thought occurred to Fitch at this point, vanishing porter aside, how seemingly untroubled this whole escapade had been so far. For a man like Fitch with the scars of brutal action littering his body, this smooth passage seemed more suspicious than a serious of fraught gun battles. Vehicles and rendezvous were always on time and in the designated locations, official documents had always been in order, staff only too happy to help and then leave him to his own devices. In short, it stank! He would be only too happy when it was all over and he could return to more, how would you put it, physically demanding opportunities for reward.

The coach performed a jarring ninety-degree turn and passed through a set of wrought iron gates replete with two armed, but disinterested local militiamen. In truth, it appeared to Fitch squinting through the door slit, they seemed almost not to see them as though under some kind of spell. He had no time to consider this further as the coach juddered to a halt and a braided porter with a pillbox hat snapped his door open and stepped to one side to allow him to alight. Fitch took his time, slowly re-holstering his pistol then checking in all directions (including up) before disembarking. He was indeed on the threshold of Aerodrome Rothschild, a peculiarly gothic building resembling a grotesquely over the top cathedral far more than a mere transport hub. Fitch was gratified that the porter in this case had not vanished, but nonetheless seemed reluctant to catch his gaze. The cabbie on the other hand was all smiles, winks and doffed cap, Fitch tipped him generously and, somewhat belatedly picking up Fitch's reticence for conversation, the man departed without another word. Sensing the chance of a tip himself the porter sprung suddenly to life attempting, somewhat foolishly, to take the night bag from Fitch. With faster reflexes than you would expect of a man of his bulk Fitch pushed him back to an arm's length distance and inclined his head to indicate the boy should lead the way into the ticket hall. Chastened, but seemingly still keen for remuneration, the boy did as he was bid and Fitch stomped along behind him.

The lobby of the aerodrome was a dizzyingly high-ceilinged affair with gothic arches bending up and out of sight in all directions. Indeed the ceiling was so far distant that the chain holding the great gas-powered chandelier, swinging lazily (and very ineffectively) in the centre of the hall, seemed to disappear after forty feet or so simply into blackness. There was a single large and extremely ornately carved booth at the far side of the room with an officious looking lady in uniform standing inside. The be-hatted lad attended him all the way to this desk and lingered, gazing at the floor, presumably for his tip. Fitch dismissed him with a low growl and he scuttled away. Reaching inside his trenchcoat to yet another internal pocket Fitch withdrew a passport and official documents declaring his case to be a diplomatic bag and presented them without ceremony to the attendant. Looking up only to match his grizzled face to a similarly dog-eared photograph in an entirely real, but extremely fictional, passport the lady barely glanced at them.

'Monsieur 'as a private flight, oui?' Fitch nodded curtly in agreement. 'Very well, ze ornithopter hangers are B11 to B17.' He nodded again, fully knowledgeable of the hanger he required. 'Monsieur is aware that there are severe weight restrictions?'

'I am,' he growled, already growing bored with the conversation.

'Tres bien monsieur, the secure lockers are through the doors to the left.' With that she stamped his passport with more force than strictly necessary, returned his documents and pulled closed a fabric shutter with the word "FERME" printed on it in bold letters barely missing his fingertips. It seemed that the customs formalities were concluded.

Fitch found himself entirely alone in the vast echoing chamber and took the moment to return his documents from whence they had come and dry swallow another of his pills from the ornate tin. At that moment the doors to which he had been directed moved fractionally and Fitch realised that someone had been watching him through the small stained glass windows. His feelings of anxiety flooded back through him as he turned and rapidly advanced on the doors, his right hand already twitching towards his pistol. Without ceremony he barged through the swing doors to find a corridor stretching for thirty feet or so. At the end of this corridor a man in black velvet jacket and dress trousers paused briefly and looked back at him without particular emotion. Fitch was shocked to see the same ornately moustachioed face, cowled in tight black curls that had caught his eye so briefly on the station platform. His pistol was out of its holster in a single breath, but the man had already moved out of sight around the corner. He charged after him, ready now for the action that he had craved for so many days. It can only have taken a second or two for him to traverse the wooden panelled corridor and turn the corner, glistening gun at the ready, senses fully heightened, pulse racing, adrenaline coursing. But as he rounded the corner to a large square room Fitch nearly choked as he found the man had once again vanished without a trace. No chance of putting this one down to a trick of the light or fatigue; the man with the distinctive facial features was simply gone.   Fitch spun desperately around, pointing his silvered pistol in all directions and clutching his precious case tightly to his side, but the windowless room presented only a façade of dusty closed lockers. The only exit door on the most distant wall was closed and had a hand bolt thrown on the near side. No presence, no man, nothing. Fitch felt his knees weaken slightly, his breath refusing to come in anything other than short stabs. Urgency was his only thought now, unholy forces were abroad and he wanted to be gone with all haste. He switched his pistol to his left hand, allowing the case to swing free, and unlocked the nearest locker. Frantically he deposited his night bag, second pistol, holsters and anything else that he could remove from his coat including some of the armour plates. The coat itself he was unable to remove due to the padlocked case, but all other items of weight were deposited. Finally, and most reluctantly, he placed his other large barrelled pistol in the locker and withdrew instead the smaller automatic gun. It would have to suffice. He closed and secured the locker stuffing the key in his pocket, unbolted the door and made his way with unseemly haste out onto the blustery airfield.

The field was vast and as deserted as the rest of the terminus. In all directions barely a handful of small craft were visible, with most hanger doors resolutely shut. Either the ungodly hour or the increasingly foul weather or more likely both was discouraging all but the foolhardiest of aviators today. Fitch could only pray that his pilot was one of these fools and his machine was fuelled and ready to fly. The most cursory of signs detailed in which direction the various hangers lay and Fitch made his way quickly, glancing all the while around for another sighting of the apparition haunting him today. He need not have concerned himself with the punctuality of his rendezvous, like everything else on this mission the pilot and craft awaited outside the appointed hanger door. The ornithopter itself was a quite magnificent contraption. A silvered pod barely big enough for two souls was the head to a massive diesel engined body straddled by two colossal articulated wings. He saw the pilot too in a reassuring homeland uniform, flying cap already on and silk scarf wrapped tightly around his face busying himself with starting the stripped-back but still powerful looking engine. It came to life with a roar and a thick black belch of acrid diesel smoke whilst the real feathers on the wing edges rippled in the gusts of wind making the vehicle look almost alive. Nearing the plane on the side indicated by the pilot Fitch made a revolution again, his small gun out in front, to make sure that there was to be no final surprise attack, but narry a soul was visible on the airpark. The craft had the markings he was told to expect and he did not hesitate to squeeze himself into the pod and proceed to buckle himself in, keeping the pistol as ready for action as he could. The pilot completed his pre-flight checks and entered the cabin on the far side with a nod. Other than a return of this gesture Fitch neither did nor said anything to keep him from his work, lest he delay their departure in any way. The last action of the pilot before entering had been to remove the chocks and aided by the squalls the machine was already in motion, the mighty engine now grinding so loudly that conversation would have been all but impossible anyway. The engine smoked heavily and Fitch found he had to cover his own face with his sleeve to prevent himself choking.

The magnificent flying machine bumped forward and creaked alarmingly as the pilot gunned the engine and turned the craft head-on into the wind. Finally when enough ground speed was attained the pilot pulled one of the myriads of levers and the full breadth of the wings was unfurled. With one enormous flap of the mechanism they were airborne and turning sharply to begin to use the wind for accelerated lift. The cabin jerked and bounced with each awesome sweep of the wings making it hard for Fitch to see if anyone was observing their departure. He fancied he made out a face in one of the hanger windows, but he might easily have imagined it as the plane lurched stomach-churningly sideways. Fitch though relaxed a little as with only four or five more beats of its magnificent wings the ornithopter had them out over the coast and well on their way to the homeland.

It was during one of these great lurching manoeuvres that the pilot's silk scarf slipped a little and with a sudden cold dread Fitch thought he saw the barest hint of a black curled moustache above his lips. Fear and anxiety surged through his veins, and with the worst possible timing his pistol slipped from his suddenly sweaty and shaking fingers and clattered into the oily footwell. With desperation he lunged after it as the craft jolted violently in the opposing direction. It stayed just out of reach of his outstretched fingers and rattled around on the grated iron floor. The craft veered so far it nearly tipped over and Fitch found himself staring straight down at the cold black waters of the channel now several thousand feet below. He fought back the urge to throw up and with every ounce of remaining strength extended his fingers to touch, then gradually ease into his palm the fallen weapon. Another alarming lurch and a great surge in height forced him back into the seat once more, but this time pistol in hand. Straining hard against the surging motion of the 'thopter and the g-forces tugging on his torso he turned to confront his companion.

But the pilot was gone.

III

High Cliffs Tea Rooms

'Oh flipper-de-jig I am completely lost,' exspluttered Reggie Peabody to no one in particular since, indeed, no one was paying him the slightest attention. Somewhere between the overpriced air taxi and the over-heated Mongolian Barbeque he had taken a seriously wrong fork in the corridor and was now unlikely to make his dinner reservation. 'Oh flipper-de-jig,' he muttered again, turning about face and wondering if retracing his steps to the Polish delicatessen might help in any way at all. Mind you the somewhat partially well named High Cliffs Tea Rooms was, quite frankly, a very easy place to get lost in. Set over some twenty or so storeys on the outside, and much more besides on the inside, of an imposing white cliff at the very end of the homeland, it was very much the place to dine. Assuming, naturally, you had the money, desire and navigation skills required to reach the restaurant of your choice. 'This really is too much,' he sighed, regretting now his decision not to ask for directions at Bellisima Italiana when a kindly maître d' had offered to assist. 'They really should have guides or something in this place.' Barely had these words escaped his lips when a head popped out of a previously hidden serving hatch and asked,

'Are you in need of assistance sir?' The voice, and head, belonged to what gave every appearance of being a teenaged girl wearing a rather natty fur-trimmed porter's jacket and matching pillbox hat. Before Reggie could so much as gather his thoughts the face continued, 'I am at your service.' The hatch in question turned out to be merely the top half of a cunningly concealed door, wallpapered in the same peculiar flock design as the rest of the corridor, which now swung fully open to reveal the young lady in her entirety. The girl sported cropped, boyish blonde hair beneath the hat, which rounded off her, not at all unpleasant if a little over eager, features including a particularly fine chin. Smart, but obviously homemade, black trousers and highly polished but clearly second hand shoes, completed the look. 'Ellen's the name, Ellen Hall. Are you lost?' She pointed an accusatory finger, 'I can certainly help you, oh please do let me!' This last plaintive exclamation caused Reggie to furrow one hairy eyebrow,

'Now see here; are you an official guide?' The girl squirmed slightly and shifted on her heels.

'Well not official as such, but I know this place better than anyone. Oh do let me help, I've memorised all the menus.' She smiled as convincingly as anyone had ever smiled and Reggie felt himself soften to her a little. To buy some time before replying he reached into his waistcoat pocket and pulled out his brass pocket watch. Nonchalantly flicking open the cover he glanced askance at the time, the revelation of which caused him to jerk alarmingly upright and turn slightly pale.

'Do you know Pierre's?' he gulped through gritted teeth, barely able to get the words out.

'Brasserie or bistro,' chirped Ellen, determined to be of maximum usefulness.

'Brasserie,' gulped Reggie suddenly feeling really rather faint.

'Yep, certainly do,' grinned Ellen, 'you're about ten floors away and on completely the wrong side, but I certainly know it, yes siree, keine problemo. Tell me though, when exactly is your reservation?'

'Oh dear god,' inhaled Reggie, 'barely twenty minutes'.

With this Ellen's face lost a little of its rosy ebullience also, but without a moment's hesitation she reached back through the door, grabbed a ragged over-stuffed leather bag, flung it over her shoulder, took his hand and headed off down the corridor with a somewhat bemused Reggie in tow.

'Then we'll talk on the move.'

Now I cannot imagine for one half of one split picosecond that you, dear reader, have not heard of Pierre's Brasserie Cordon Bleu Haute Cuisine de Haute Falaise? Non? I mean no? Oh come now. It is a place of such pompously overhyped provenance that it requires booking no less than one year and three months in advance and arrival within eighty seconds (no more, and certainly no less) of your reservation or your booking will be handed, without ceremony, to the salivating head of the queue in the returnee's lounge. Yes an entire lounge, devoted to such purpose. Not only that, but the stigma of missing a sitting at Pierre's will haunt you, and no doubt seventy times seven generations of your descendants thereafter. Assuming of course you have the wherewithal to overcome your embarrassment and social stigmatisation enough to actually find a mate and reproduce at all. It is the place to be, the place to be seen, *the* name to drop in both polite and impolite society and, without doubt, somewhere not to be missed in your small, short and fragile lifetime. I hear the food's not that bad either.

'Tell me sir, if I may call you sir, how exactly did you come to be on the rather lesser frequented Outer Mongolian and Slavic range of the tea rooms, this rather middling of Summer evenings?' ventured Ellen as they moved with unseemly haste down a myriad of higgledy-piggledy corridors dodging waiters and porters at every turn. 'Air taxi or boat bus?'

'Air taxi,' gasped Reggie, finding the pace somewhat harder to manage given his portly frame. Ellen exhaled a large sigh,

'Then they've ripped you off mightily sir. If you should ever manage to locate said cabbie again, I would most assuredly ask for your money back.'

'Fat chance,' muttered Reggie, swerving with no little elegance (he put it down to his dancehall training) to avoid three Sherpa manhandling large, unrecognisable, slabs of meat in the opposite direction. At least the corridor here was a little wider than when they had first met although it struck Reggie that they seemed to be leaving the eating establishments behind. 'Do you really know where you are going?' He enquired tentatively. Before she had a chance to reply they came to a halt beside a pair of functional looking swing doors marked very clearly with a large sign reading – "Staff Only - No Patrons Beyond This Point" underneath this was written in slightly larger writing "WITHOUT EXCEPTION" and finally below that someone had added the words "That totally means you!" in red ink, underlined twice. Ellen pulled him close by his dress shirt collar and whispered conspiratorially,

'I most certainly do sir. The question is though,' she paused dramatically, 'do you trust me?'

Reggie gulped hard, looked at Ellen, at the door and back at Ellen again. He thought of his reservation and the seconds that were ticking away whilst he pondered the question. In the end he gulped again, 'I do.'

'Really? Oh splendid,' chirped Ellen, sounding somewhat surprised. 'Then let's tarry no longer with silly questions.' And with that she pulled him, waistcoat, watch chain and all through the service doors and into the starkly lit corridor beyond.

They had entered the labyrinth of service tunnels, lifts and miscellaneous ancillary rooms that served the great High Cliffs complex. Reggie felt quite awestruck as they dodged nimbly, and at some pace, past a myriad of chefs, waiters, washer folk, bakers, butchers, probably the odd candlestick maker and endless streams of food porters, all heading this way and that with such focus and determination that they seemed oblivious to all else around them and, despite the fact that the red-faced rotund gentlemen following the resolute and eager teenage waif made for quite an odd coupling, no one paid them the slightest attention. Progress was reassuringly swift and Reggie found himself day dreaming just a little; he pictured himself being ushered towards his seat by fragrant waiters, the reassuringly heavy menu being placed in his hand, the starched napkin pulled across his lap. He fancied he could almost smell the divine Chablis, almost taste the legendary succulent minute steak...

With a mighty bump Reggie was brought back to earth as Ellen slammed him up against a wall of lockers and bid him stay silent with a single finger to her lips and sharp 'Shhh'. Holding his gaze with her finger she melodramatically swept her hand round until both it and Reggie's view were directed to the opposite wall of the lobby. Quite a scene presented itself. The whole opposite wall appeared to be some sort of giant larder or storage room into which a stream of regimented porters was stacking all kinds of foodstuffs. Wooden crates of who knows what here, stacked carcasses of a whole wildlife park of animals there. The room was easily forty feet square and was very nearly stacked to the gunnels. At either side of this space were two mighty concertinaed doors with a vast array of hydraulic and hissing steam-powered pistons to govern their movement. Next to these doors stood attendants in crisp blue overalls, clipboards in hand noting all the toing's and froing's with stern attention.

'Behold,' incanted Ellen in an entirely unnecessary stage whisper, given the din emanating from the room, 'Medium Chilled Service Elevator (East Side) Number 3.' Staring further Reggie realised that the somewhat prosaically-named apparatus was indeed a giant lift, which was nearing maximum capacity as the queue of porters began to tail off and engineers could be seen readying themselves to one side of the doors.

'Now,' intoned Ellen again in subdued voice, 'we have to get on this if we are to have any chance of making your reservation. Slight problem is that no people are allowed on board.' Reggie looked wide-eyed at her.

'So what are you suggesting, I disguise myself as a box of fruit?'

'Don't be so silly,' she chided reaching into her large leather bag and retrieving a carefully folded white sheet and a small cardboard tube sealed at both ends. 'I'll create a diversion, then we'll simply walk on and hide ourselves under this sheet.' At this Reggie somehow managed to conjure up a look that was even more sceptical than his previous one,

'Oh far less silly I'm sure.' She ignored this implied slight and carried on, 'when I say go. Well - go!' With this she snapped off the end of the tube, reversed it and struck a previously hidden wick. The device began to fizz alarmingly. 'Not yet!' she barked as Reggie became more than a little twitchy. She began to count down, 'Five, four, three...' then with great strength she threw the tube to the far side of the room beyond where the engineers where gathered.

'Aren't you supposed to wait for one?' spluttered Reggie. At that exact moment the firecracker exploded in a shower of sparks and began to smoke heavily and all faces turned towards the commotion.

'Now!' cried Ellen and set off towards the slowly closing lift doors.

'I thought the word was go?' protested Reggie, but he quickly caught her up and just as the great iron doors were a few feet apart they shimmied in between and collapsed on a handy stack of Satsuma boxes. Quick as you like Ellen flung the large sheet over them both. All of this had gone unnoticed as one of the engineers attended the now spent firework with an oversized fire extinguisher on a little cart and the others looked on tut-tutting like this sort of thing happened everyday and was frankly just another one of those nuisances that one must grin and bear. Under the sheet the two of them heard the doors clang shut and mechanisms begin to whirr both beneath and above them. Ellen let the sheet drop, the temperature in the lift was somewhat arctic and their breath came out in clouds of vapour.

'See, easy as that,' she breathed through already chattering teeth, 'hope you don't mind a little c-cold?'

'D-d-d-do I-I-I have any ch-ch-ch-choice?' stuttered Reggie in reply; Ellen assumed the question was rhetorical. Nevertheless perhaps she could take time for a situation update whilst they waited for the lift to ascend to its destination.

'This lift will t-t-t-take us up f-f-five floors,' she began. 'Then we c-c-c-cut through the l-l-l-llivestock m-m-m-market...'

'l-l-l-llivestock m-m-m-market?!'

'Yes, there are four m-m-m-markets in High C-c-c-Cliffs. Livestock, fish, groceries and ch-ch-ch-cheese.'

'Ch-ch-ch-cheese?' emitted Reggie and then promptly decided to give up talking and concentrate on staying warm.

'Yes, ch-ch-ch-cheese.' At this point Ellen also decided to give up trying to explain and began to fold away the sheet. The towering piles of chilled produce around them began to tremble slightly as the ascent of the lift began to slow. Ellen hopped off the Orange boxes and motioned for him to stand close, although the vibrating of the lift made this a little tricky.

'Wh-wh-when the door opens, f-f-f-follow me. Don't h-h-h-hesitate or look around. G-g-g-got it?' She gave him her sternest look.

'R-r-r-right oh.' Was all that Reggie could offer as the lift juddered to a halt and he had to reach up with his arm to prevent a box of frozen egg powder landing on their heads. There was no time for further preparations as the door began to creak open and the chatter from the waiting porters began to filter in.

'Go!' yelled Ellen, and they were off. Straight through the barely wide enough gap in the doors into the maelstrom of porters with trolleys and stewards with clipboards on the other side. Ignoring all the *Oi*s and *You there*s and *I Say*s they bumped and bundled their way through and down a handy service corridor. Although clearly put out, everyone in the lobby appeared to have better things to do that run after a generously proportioned gentleman and an urchin who had decided to stowaway on a goods lift. One steward did squeak up a technically correct, but really rather superfluous 'No people allowed y'know' but by that point they were round another corner and practically out of earshot.

'I say,' grinned Reggie, his ruddy colour slowly leaching back to join a smile easing its way across his face, 'what a jolly wheeze.'

'You haven't seen anything yet,' muttered Ellen, who was somewhat relieved that Reggie didn't seem to hear.

A few paces beyond the sixth corner, or was it the seventh, the corridor stretched out for nearly a hundred yards or so with no other soul in sight. The chaos of the lift lobby was no longer audible and the only sounds that accompanied them were the clump of their boots on the stone floor and the low hiss of the occasional gas lamp on the wall. With this short lull from the hectic nature of their journey so far, and daring to believe that they might make the reservation at Pierre's after all, Reggie decided he'd get a thing or two off his chest.

'Y'know Ellen, there are two things that are puzzling me.' She gave him a little look as if to say "oh yeah?" but he ignored this completely. 'The first is the circumstances by which a young lady such as yourself came to be wandering these corridors.' He held up a hand to prevent her from interjecting at this point, 'but that can, if you permit me, wait until later as firstly I would like to invite you to join me for a hearty supper.' She seemed about to protest but he halted her again, 'No buts! Whether we make it in time or not, although I do pray we do, we shall dine somewhere and you will be my guest.' She gave a little shrug, but said nothing. 'Good, it's settled. Now the other thing that you might be able to cast some light on, is why this bally place is called the High Cliffs Tea Rooms? I mean I get the High Cliffs bit, but where is the tea room?'

'Ah now,' piped up Ellen, 'that I do know. Legend has it that once upon a time a little old lady called Miss Myrtle set up a tea room at High Cliff to serve the few day trippers that meandered that way and give her somewhere to fulfil her retirement dream of spending all day baking and brewing. After a year or two it became so popular that it seemed to make sense to add a restaurant to cater for those after heartier fare. Rather than build a new establishment next door they accomplished this by extending on the side of the original building. This process continued and one by one, piece by piece, year on year other restaurateurs decided to jump on the bandwagon and add more and more eateries to cater for the changing tastes of the, by now, plentiful tourists. Then as night follows day, the service industries came also; a laundrette here, a greengrocer there, florists, butchers, bakers, cake makers, until after many years the whole complex we are now traversing came into being. It's changed so many times and in so many ways that the only thing linking it back to its origins is its name. Eventually poor Miss Myrtle passed away and her teashop closed, but out of respect to her and what had grown from her idea no one else ventured to step into the teashop business but rather let it be always associated with her. Over time and many more re-designs and re-builds the location of the original tea room has been lost, in fact to this day, no one knows where it originally stood, although there are plenty of mad theories as where it might have been.'

'Well I never,' muttered Reggie, 'who'd have thought? Y'know I'm a bit of an entrepreneur myself and I was contemplating opening my own establishment here, I can see that your knowledge might come in rather...' His voice tailed off at this point and his nose and indeed whole face began to wrinkle in displeasure, 'I say, what's that terrible smell?'

'Ah, that,' began Ellen whilst rummaging in her bag to retrieve a pair of large clothes pegs, 'is the great Eastern Cliff Livestock Market.' With that she popped a clothes peg on her nose and offered the other to Reggie. He took it readily and snapped it over his bulbous nose with haste.

'hats not uch etter,' he intoned through bunged up nose, 'I an till mell it!' he added and pretty soon he could hear it too. A great cacophony of animal noises hit him square in the chops as they came through another set of swinging doors and found themselves on a vast wooden balcony, looking down onto the most incredible subterranean (or indeed terranean) animal market he had ever clapped eyes on. The noise was ear-bursting: quacking, oinking, braying, mooing; and the smell quite overpowering. The, by now, ubiquitous stream of white-coated porters, tall-hatted chefs and other miscellaneous officials was attending the many animal pens. Battalions of sheep, ducks, cows and goats and who knew what else were being chivvied and herded and flocked, and whatever one did with goats, through thoroughfares between the pens. Auctions where being held loudly at every corner and for a second Reggie thought he might faint as all his senses were quite overloaded. In the end there was no time for any of that carry on as Ellen grabbed his arm and dragged him down some stairs and right into the thick of it. Whilst carefully trying to avoid the heaving throng of animal life and being careful not to tread in anything too effluent looking, Reggie hurried along behind, keen to get this leg of the escapade behind them as soon as possible. After a few moments the exit for which they were heading came into sight, but before they could reach it, Ellen diverted them and came to a stop beside an animal pen.

'Guy a goat!' she instructed pointing at the pen.

'Eh?' muttered Reggie unable to understand what she was on about; he accompanied this with what he hoped was a suitably confused looking shrug of the shoulders.

'Guy a goat!' exclaimed Ellen again, but realising this was getting nowhere plucked her clothes peg from her nose, 'Buy a goat, buy a goat!"

'Buy a goat?' spluttered Reggie doing likewise, 'whatever for?'

'Or a duck or a chicken or something,' added Ellen urging him to reach for his wallet. Before he could ask for additional reasoning she provided it anyway, 'we have one last trip to make, up the final few floors, but to make it we need to take a livestock air taxi, and for that you need...'

'Livestock,' Reggie finished the sentence for her and with a somewhat resigned air he reached for his wallet.

Negotiations were quickly concluded, for Reggie was certainly not short of a bob or two. Then the odd couple replete with a slightly over excitable nanny goat in tow made a rapid exit of the market and headed direct for the livestock taxis.

The High Cliffs Tea Rooms had two air corridors cleared for airship traffic. To the west the patrons arrived fully suited and booted looking to be deposited as near as possible, or as in poor unfortunate Reggie's case, as far as possible, from their chosen eating establishment. The East side, where they were just emerging back into the warm evening sunlight, was primarily reserved for service vessels, and the livestock market floor in particular was served by a bobbing fleet of airship taxis dedicated solely to transporting livestock between the many floors. Now when I say fleet I am perhaps overplaying it a smidge since, as it was nearly the end of the day, there were a mere two airships awaiting possible trade and they appeared to be vying with each other for who's was the scruffiest vessel. Reggie was less concerned with this lack of choice than with the rickety walkway - suspended only with a handful of old ropes - onto which they had to venture, goat and all. As they wobbled their way somewhat less than surefootedly along this air bridge Reggie tried not to look down the two hundred or so feet that encompassed the many wings of the Tea Rooms below them and the peaking surf of the channel at the very bottom of the cliff. Away to the east the beautiful white homeland cliffs stretched out as far as they could see and the great, elongated shadows of the Tea Rooms played across them as the late summer sun warmed their backs. Glancing sideways, to avoid looking down, Reggie saw the big round clock that hung over the entrance to the market and with some astonishment realised they still had two whole minutes in hand.

'I say, how far have we left to go?' ventured Reggie trying not to sound too excited as they tugged on the goat's rope to encourage its passage into the fractionally less shabby of the two air taxis. Pausing from her exertions to pass the goat's rope to the sleepy looking cabbie, Ellen looked up and pointed with her free hand.

'See for yourself,' she announced with more than a hint of triumph in her voice. Reggie did as he was bid and just six or so stories up, beyond the garish neon of the American "Eat Me" diner and the rather less flamboyant Ye Olde Authentic Nepalese Buffet sign was a rather plain looking wooden service door with a simple painted board that read "Pierre's - Tradesmen Only". Catching sight of this Reggie felt his heart leap, his pulse quicken, his soul sing and his foot miss the last step completely sending him somersaulting forward into the now untethered airship and directly onto both Ellen and their more than somewhat startled goat. The goat kicked out, as well it

49

might, and caught the distracted airship pilot right in the *how's your father!* This in turn propelled him backwards in the gondola, and the fending pole he'd been using struck the envelope of the balloon and an alarming hissing sound accompanied by a disturbing, if gradual, lessening of altitude began to occur. Reggie's exclamation at this point, alas, cannot be printed. As the pilot struggled to regain his feet and attend to ballast and balloon Ellen moved somewhat more speedily. Quick as the proverbial flash she delved into her bag again and to Reggie's complete astonishment, and no little alarm, extracted a rather nifty looking handgun with a brass harpoon loaded in the barrel. Into this she inserted and clamped the end of a handy mooring rope and took aim high above them. With a barking crack of gunpowder the harpoon and pursuing rope snaked rapidly up into the air; the other end she passed around her waist and threw the final length urgently in Reggie's direction. 'Hang on for dear life!' she exclaimed and just as Reggie took hold of the rope it went taut and the airship gondola floor dropped away from under them. By this point they both had every limb wrapped around the rope that seemed, by some miracle, to be holding tight. How long *they* could hang on for was another matter entirely. In these few seconds Ellen had not ceased her action, she discarded the harpoon gun and in its place retrieved a complicated looking clockwork thingy-me-bob about the size of box camera, and before Reggie could ask what the dickens it was, she expertly clamped it around the rope and then pulled down four slim rubber-coated handles on the sides of the mechanism. 'Grab a handle!' she instructed. Reggie complied and found the grips to be firm and much easier to hold than the rope. He then looked on bemused as Ellen inserted a large brass key into the mechanism and began to frantically wind. 'Now, whatever happens, DO NOT LET GO OF THE HANDLES!' bellowed Ellen.

'Why?!' screamed Reggie, 'what's going to...' again his question was cut dead as Ellen ceased winding and with a flick of a sturdy looking switch the mechanism began to rapidly climb up the rope, dragging the two dangling miscreants along with it. 'Well I say!' gasped Reggie, kind of, as they sped ever upwards. Just as Reggie fancied he was catching the faintest whiff of freshly baked baguette and only seconds after the astonished diners of Eat Me watched open-mouthed as they scuttled past – disaster struck! A strong gust of wind blew them out from the building and into a stomach-churning near horizontal orientation. Reggie could mutter no oaths this time as the air was beaten from his lungs and it was all he could do to keep both hands on the still-climbing clockwork pulley.

For a split second the wind eased and they found themselves briefly motionless in this reclining position. During this calm interlude Reggie noted that the air taxi they had left was now buoyant again some hundred feet below them and had began to chug back towards them with the goat standing calmly, as if she were a figurehead, on the very prow of the gondola. Before he could contemplate this further the lull ended and they began to swing back with gathering speed towards the building. At this point Reggie determined to clamp his eyes tight shut and offer up any prayer he could recall. With his eyes closed he failed to see that they were heading directly for a giant billboard with a large poster for *Bert's Original Coach Inn Café* and, presumably, the very face of Bert himself looming some twelve feet tall, plastered across it. Their trajectory was sending them straight for Bert's beaming mouth and they hit it full on with all their force. It barely needs saying that both Reggie and Ellen were astonished that they did not bounce off the hoarding, but instead plunged right through it, ripping the paper in all directions. They continued to swing through a half opened doorway hidden by the poster and then were dumped unceremoniously onto the floor of a long abandoned room. Dust and disused cutlery had flown in all directions as they landed and it took them a few moments to recover their breath and get their bearings again. When they did it became apparent they had been deposited in what appeared to be the *Marie Celeste* of cafes, set with just four tables, chintzy doilies, napkins and china plates still laid out for would be diners. It was much as if when the last customer had paid their bill the owner had simply locked the door and left, leaving everything just as it was. Ellen and Reggie gazed around them in a complete daze; both the literal and metaphorical air had been sucked from them and they were beginning to feel their bruises with every dust-induced cough.

They were brought out of their reverie by a long "Baaaaah" and looked back at the doorway and the shafts of light streaming through the torn edges of the poster, to see a cheery goat face, followed by the ruddier cheeks of the taxi-pilot peering in to see if they were still in one piece.

'Well my very goodness me,' offered the airman fixing his landing hook onto the doorframe and pulling his airship up against the billboard. 'What on earth have we here?' He too was gazing around the freshly revealed interior. By this point a winded, but still energised Ellen had gingerly picked herself up and came face to face with the goat busy chewing something it had nabbed from one of the twee tables. Curious she reached out to tug the item from its mouth, brushed it clean of dust and goat saliva with her sleeve and held it towards the light coming from the old doorway,

'Well I never,' she breathed almost unable to speak.

'What is it my dear?' coughed Reggie trying to clear his throat. Without another word she turned the menu around and where she had wiped the dirt you could see in very flowery lettering, but as plain as the nose on your face, the words: "Miss Myrtle's High Cliffs Tea Room".

'Well I blinking never,' muttered Reggie quite astonished; all thoughts of the delights of Pierre's Brassiere now extinguished from his mind. And truth be told dear reader, little did he know that with this astonishingly unlikely discovery both he and Ellen's lives would never be quite the same again.

Postscript

This story is key in explaining why Reggie Peabody – later Lord Reginald of High Cliffs – eccentric, millionaire and founder of the Miss Myrtle's Tea Rooms franchise came to always keep a pet goat.

Ellen Hall went on to become a renowned and glamorous explorer; she is also credited with patenting the Hall's Handheld Harpoon and Clockwork Climbing Contraption.

IV

A Christmas Carry-On

(With profuse apologies to Charles Dickens)

The potential-time-displacing-thermogromitide-compostulator was dead, to begin with. There is no doubt whatever about that. Marley on the other hand, was in rude health and chose this moment to swing a somewhat desultory steel toe-capped boot at this aforementioned component, which gave forth a most baleful clang in return. It was after all a fairly chunky piece of mostly ferrous equipment. The noise of this crude admonishment brought Marley's master and fellow inventor scurrying into the room.

'Whatever is the commotion dear boy?' inquired the newcomer carrying what was most probably his third goblet of mulled wine of the evening, for indeed this very night was Christmas Eve. Sebastian Crumplefold Rouge, known to all and their spouses as Scrouge, cut a somewhat more casual figure than Marley since he had already donned his second best dressing gown and a tasselled nightcap and was in the full throws of making most merry. He ran a calloused hand through his mince pie crumb inflected moustache and shook his head in mild despair.

'Marley old thing, you'll do yourself a mischief. It's Christmas Eve join me for a pie and some punch.' He waved a gowned arm in the vague direction of the parlour where a roaring log fire could be heard crackling heartily. Marley, hands on the hips of his crumpled coat continued to stare at the machine that was now sparking in a slightly pathetic way. Eventually, after what seemed an age, he lifted his greasy welding goggles from his eyes and turned to face Scrouge, his face lightly smeared with oil. Unlike Scrouge, Marley was attired in full-length, heavy-duty brown cotton lab coat (heavily creased) insulated leather gauntlets (well soiled) and the aforementioned work boots (complete with recently added dent on the right toe). None of these however was his most distinctive feature, which was instead a shock of white hair caused by a somewhat unfortunate incident with a 20,000 Volt static electricity generator, a size 12 plumbers' wrench and a ferret. Best not to ask.

'I don't know how you can always be so blasted jolly,' he accused Scrouge. 'This Time-Machine of ours isn't really going to invent itself now, is it?' Certainly on current viewing the room full of machinery gave no indication of forming itself spontaneously into a functioning time machine. However it was quite a picture: pipes and mechanisms festooned every wall, linked by wires, induction loops and controls the like of which you'd have never seen before. In truth there were far too many eccentric contraptions in the room for me to do it justice on these meagre pages. However, just off centre in the room was a particularly distinctive arrangement that certainly drew the eye. Its main constituents were a giant brass oval made of chunky pipework easily big enough to allow a medium-sized donkey to pass through without major impediment. Directly behind this was a large, smoked glass bell-chamber with a wrought iron door that could easily accommodate one person and perhaps a second with only a little discomfort on their part. All the other crazy devices, including miscellaneous valves and control panels all seemed focussed on this central orifice. The very cold heart of the entirely non-functioning apparatus, as Marley had never described it.

'Oh, *our* time machine is it now,' chuckled Scrouge to himself with a part rueful, part sozzled smile. 'Sometimes I think you get ideas a little above your station Marley old chap.' Accompanied by more slow head-shaking Scrouge turned away from Marley heading back to his supper. 'I'm away to bed soon, tomorrow is Christmas for heaven's sake, go home and spend this sacred eve with your kin. Oh, and don't bother coming in tomorrow either.' He paused at the oak doorway to raise his now somewhat tepid mulled wine in a toast and a simple benediction: 'Merry Christmas Marley – do try to enjoy a little of the spirit of the season.' With that he swept, a little drunkenly, out of the laboratory, colliding with the doorpost only the once, and disappeared to enjoy as many of the spirits of the season as he could squeeze in before bedtime.

With this overly dramatic departure it was Marley's turn to shake his head and offer a particularly unmemorable: 'Christmas, bah sauerkraut'.

With Scrouge gone and the laboratory starting to turn a little chilly as the frosts of the evening scratched their icy fingers down the window, Marley conceded that perhaps the old man was right for a change. There was little he could do that evening and since the indefatigably jovial buffoon had given all the laboratory assistants Christmas day off there was bugger all to be done tomorrow also. With a heavy heart and cold extremities he began to do as little as possible to tidy the laboratory before departing himself.

It was at that exact moment that something rather unexpected occurred; heralded by a cloud of sparking steam that materialised as if from the very elements themselves. There followed a flash of light and a clap of thunder the sheer force of which threw Marley off his feet and into a nearby workbench scattering a clatter of tools in all directions. When the steam began to dissipate and Marley had regained what little composure he had to take in the situation he felt himself feeling more than a little queasy. If his hair had not already been pure white it would almost certainly have become so due to the sheer shock of it all. In fact Marley did tentatively raise a hand to his locks just to confirm that his hair hadn't decided to add insult to injury and fall out completely. He wouldn't put it past it.

The scene that now confronted Marley's watery, blinking eyes was quite extraordinary. In the centre of the room directly opposite the large brass oval, was a second similarly constructed, if a little more tarnished, brass loop; and behind that a second over-sized glass bell jar. The two were like bizarre mirror images of each other except that new arrival was the more worn and seemingly world-weary of the two. Waving the last of the smoke away the trembling Marley tentatively began to approach the door of the apparition. Could it be true, did the blasted time machine turn out to be a workable proposition after all now visiting its creators from the future? Or perhaps some other horrors lay within? Marley's knees began to shake uncontrollably as the iron door of the bell jar creaked open and a hooded figure stepped out of the glass compartment through the brass ring and into the laboratory. Marley by this point was a quivering mess 'Oh baleful traveller from the future be you gentle upon me,' he wailed pathetically. 'This being Christmas an' all,' he added in case this had any bearing on his fate.

'Oh pull yourself together you great blithering pansy!' admonished a very familiar sounding voice. As the figure folded back the hood of his cloak Marley found he was staring into his own, somewhat phlegmier, eyes as the stranger gave every impression of being none other than an older version of himself. Indeed the more he looked the truer it became; the hair was the same white shock, if a little thinner on top. The face the same mess of features, if you glossed over the few additional wrinkles and a liver spot or three. Mind you he did seem to have put on a little weight, although this was amply covered by a very fine waistcoat trimmed in gold. A particularly vulgar, chunky watch chain completed the visage and even the cloak he wore looked like a particularly expensive garment.

Now dear reader, at this point in the story I should warn you that attempting to follow a time-travelling narrative of this type in words is akin to juggling a dozen or so particularly frisky and soaking wet (perhaps also lightly oiled) otters whilst attempting to complete The Bumper Times Christmas Crossword on your lap with a frustratingly blunt pencil. In an attempt to assist you in this, **ALMOST IMPOSSIBLE**, endeavour I will henceforth refer to Marley as, well: "Marley" and the more aged plumper version as: "Old Marley" or some variation on this. I hope this helps somewhat, although I really wouldn't blame you if you threw in the proverbial towel at this point and gave up the whole shebang as a bad lot. For the brave amongst you who choose to hang on in there, I will forge on.

'Quiet now you blathering nincompoop!' thundered Old Marley again and Marley thought it best to comply. 'I don't really know how all this time travel malarkey works, but I cannot imagine that us meeting in this way is something generally understood to be pukka. Do you get my drift?' Marley The Less Old nodded although he was somewhat shy of the drift at that particular instance. 'Fine, so it is what it is and it is crucial to our future prosperity and y'know happiness and such that you listen to this tale and comply with every last detail of the instructions I am about to issue. Feel free to make yourself a little more comfortable, but don't get too close in case this has unforeseen consequences, I'll make this a brief as I can.'

With this Marley The Younger sat himself on the floor and Marley The Elder presented his scenario. The long and short of it being thus: the time machine could (demonstrably) be made to work and it seemed that the vital breakthrough in its development came the very following morn – the twenty-fifth of December 1825 (in the new calendar) a particularly memorable date thus explaining why The Older Marley could easily recall it. Despite this singular breakthrough in the science of man and womankind alike it would take a further forty years or so to fully evolve the idea and eventually make Marley an obscenely rich and disgustingly powerful man. However there had been a rather odd occurrence when in a fit of narcissist (and somewhat drunken) conceit Old Marley had decided that his very first trip of note in the machine would be to surprise his younger self just after the eureka moment, as it were, and indulge in a little self to self gloating. On the occasion of this egomaniacal visitation that Marley The More Aged had thought would come as no great surprise to the less decrepit version (since he would know by then that time travel was possible – are you keeping up?) Old Marley discovered with horror that his younger self had been sent home on Christmas day by that bumbling ball of seasonal buffoonery – Scrouge – and the breakthrough had NOT been made! Terrified by this revelation, but somehow realising he was still "in the game" as it were, he resolved to immediately travel back to the eve of the day of days and convince the younger self to get Scrouge to come over all humbug and demand that Marley work the aforementioned holy day and allow them to make the necessary discovery.

'What?' spluttered the more juvenile of the two, hitting the nail rather squarely on the head.

'Look dunderchops,' barked Marley The Senior losing what little patience he had, 'It's blasted easy and I've done all the hard work for you.' He then proceeded to explain his plan, which seemed highly over-wrought to the more callow of the two, but Marley The More Rotund gave every impression of being about to explode so he thought best not to argue. The principle gist of the scheme seemed to be to use the time machine to convince Scrouge that Christmas was a rather over-rated event whilst simultaneously also bringing him to think that time was short and they ought to "press on" with all alacrity. The former was to be accomplished by travelling to Scrouge's childhood which, by all accounts must have been rotten as, apparently, his parents abandoned him, and from thence to the future where a quick shufty around Scrouges's own grave ought to do the job with the latter part.

'I've done a little research and the dates are all programmed in to my machine. I needn't tell you how to work it since, after all, you made it anyway,' he chuckled. With that Marley The Latter seemed done with instructions and produced a bottle of port from a leather pouch on his belt designed specifically for such a purpose (with a natty snifter also attached) and made towards the non-working version of the time machine. 'Since there with be no small amount of time-space continuum tomfoolery afoot tonight and I am not of this moment, the safest place for me would be in the bell chamber of your earlier not-yet-operational contraption where I intend to do justice by this rather nice vintage. Once I see you have accomplished the required effect I'll make good my escape taking my machine with me and all will be well.' And with that he stomped into the chamber and shut the door behind him.

And so once again Marley found himself more-or-less alone in the room despite the fact it now containing two time machines, in varying states of functionality, and a second version of himself! Given that he was still somewhat dazed and now in considerable fear of what his more ruddy version might choose to do if he didn't crack on with "the plan" he thought it prudent to do just that. The decision made, his mind calmed just a fraction and it occurred to him that what he needed was a disguise of some sort and a bit of creative melodrama to encourage Scrouge along on this tin pot adventure. Since, clearly, no amount of simple sweet-talking was going to rouse Scrouge from his slumber considering that the arrival of a *whacking great time machine from the future* in his backroom had not done so. The laboratory offered little by way of obvious assistance in this endeavour so he moved to the window for inspiration, and lo it was forthcoming. Outside moving gingerly along the icy and dimly lit pavement was a person, clearly a little the worse for drink, wearing a gaudy red Saint Nicolas costume with cheap fur trim and fake whiskers, waving a charity collecting box on a stick. Quick as you like Marley headed to the front door to intercept his quarry tarrying only to collect one of Scrouge's earlier inventions on the way out. As he opened the great front door he began preparing the contraption, which Scrouge, every bit the lovey-dovey pacifist had designed for the non-lethal detention of perpetrators by constables and such like. The device was a kind of sawn-off blunderbuss affair that fired a rubber ball of medium density with sufficient velocity to incapacitate without causing grievous injury. He cocked the flint and held the pistol behind his back whilst simultaneously waving his free arm aloft: 'My dear Santa tarry a minute.' He called out, in the most jovial tone he could muster.

'Ho ho ho,' replied Father Christmas turning a little unsteadily to face Marley, 'Cerry Mistmas to you my good man, or woman,' he slurred 'would you dare to make a conation?' Having completed his about face he jangled the collecting box optimistically.

'Kind of,' replied Marley cryptically before brandishing the pistol and firing the flintlock mechanism with a sharp crack and a puff of smoke. The rubber projectile emerged with all haste and hit Santa squarely on the chops after which he fell promptly to the deck like a floored boxer. Without so much as a "by your leave" Marley, who was relieved that the prone man was still breathing, dragged the inert body down the back alley and into Scrouge's vast coal bunker. With reasonable efficiency he removed the costume and false beard and headed forthwith back to collect a few other essential items for his ever-evolving scheme, that was almost beginning to make sense in his head.

True to form Scrouge had certainly not held back on the seasonal cheer. He had demolished the best part of a flagon of mulled wine lovingly prepared by Mrs Bestial the housekeeper and washed it down with a plateful of savoury biscuits and blue cheese, or was that the other way round? Needless to say this cheery overindulgence had had the usual effect of such things and Scrouge was now snoring rumbustiously in his most comfortable armchair near a now gently glowing fireplace. With a rude start Scrouge was suddenly woken by a sharp bang and flash in the grate (it later turned out to have been a firecracker, but at that time Scrouge was not to know). He sat bolt upright in his chair and gazed with gummed up eyes on an unholy apparition that had appeared before him as if by magic or witchcraft. Stood before him was an intimidating beast of a figure clad in red robes, a dirty beard (was it coal dust?), shiny slatted goggles covered his eyes and his hands were encased in mighty gloves with iron fingers and his legs in knee high boots with glistening buckles and straps.

'Ho ho and indeed ho!' intoned the apparition, for wont of something more insightful.

'Do not harm me oh spirit!' squeaked Scrouge who was actually mightily afeard and a smidge worried he might have a little accident, the telling of which would not be pleasant. Mercifully this did not happen. After a time which was probably only a few seconds, but seemed longer, in which the ghastly figure continued to stand menacingly but did little else besides, Scrouge felt compelled to ask, 'Is there anything I can do for you? Mulled wine perhaps?'

'Oh blow this for a game of soldiers,' muttered the figure and proceeded to produce a blunderbuss type pistol that he aimed directly at Scrouge's head.

'I say isn't that my...' Scrouge was unable to complete his question as the gun discharged violently and the rubber projectile knocked Scrouge right back to a state of unconsciousness much like where he had been only a few moments earlier.

When he came to, with the aid of some smelling salts under his ample nose, Scrouge was mystified to find that he was outside and propped up against a rough brick wall next to a window. It was still dark in the street but it seemed somehow earlier in the evening than before, which was quite unsettling. Or perhaps it was the following day; after all he had no idea how long he'd been out for. He recalled then that there had been a horrible figure and as he glanced around he was somewhat unsurprised to find that it was still there helping to hold him up against the wall. The only slight improvement on his previous situation was that the ghoul seemed to have finally got his story straight.

'I am the ghost of Christmas Past,' he bellowed at Scrouge.

'If you say so spirit,' replied Scrouge, still shaking a little, realising there was something a little familiar about the voice but in his dazed state he could not yet place it.

'I am here to teach you the real meaning of Christmas!' continued the apparition in an unnecessarily loud tone, 'and it isn't all that good.' It added, suddenly sounding not quite to sure, but still very loud.

'Fair enough,' muttered Scrouge, 'but perhaps you'd keep it down a bit, I've got a humdinger of a headache coming on.'

'Silence!' screeched the ghoul, regaining a little of its evil composure, 'Look into the window and gaze upon the miserable face of Christmas past.' As much in the hope that it would shut him up for a bit Scrouge did as he was bidden.

It took a little while for his bleary eyes to gain something approaching focus but as they did Scrouge began to make out the scene within the building that was just about lit by flickering candles. It turned out to be a schoolroom of some sort. The beaten up old desks were all empty, bar one where a lonely figure sat working away with small pieces of metal and a miniature tool kit.

'Tell me oh fateful spirit,' began Scrouge reverently, mostly for fear of a further round of shouting, 'who is this poor wretch who sits all alone?'

'Are you kidding me?' muttered the ghost and then added 'put your glasses on you old duffer.' Mildly put out by the insult, but realising that it might actually help, Scrouge reached into his dressing gown pocket and brought out his eyepieces. Suitably attired he looked again and this time the recognition was instantaneous and sent a murmur through his heart. The figure at the desk working animatedly at his construction set was none other than the younger Sebastian Crumplefold Rouge. A huge smile broke out over Scrouge's face at the realisation and he began to gibber excitedly, 'It's me it's me,' he turned to the apparition and patted him heartily on the shoulder, 'Oh spirit I have no idea how you've done it, but that's me, that's me!' he pointed excitedly 'How wonderful!'

'How wonderful!' bellowed the ghost with more than a hint of annoyance in his voice. 'What's so bloomin' wonderful about being on your own at Christmas?'

'Is it still Christmas?' inquired Scrouge 'Oh the joy! I loved this time more than any other, there were always toys to take apart and re-assemble, puzzles to ponder, word games of my invention to torment my tutors...'

'What!' the spirit seemed more than a little put out now, 'but I assumed your Christmases must have been awful, abandoned by your parents and all that.'

'Oh spirit, whoever does your research needs to be given the royal order of the boot,' teased Scrouge, but a little melancholy entered his voice. 'My parents never abandoned me, but they were elderly and had to send me away to school. Despite this I was spoilt rotten, never wanted for anything, especially at Christmas.'

'Oh for heaven's sake,' intoned the ghoul sounding really rather put out. 'Well in that case I have another announcement to make: I am now the Ghost of Christmas yet to come,' and with that he wearily raised the pistol again.

Knowing what was coming, Scrouge just sighed.

With another waft of the smelling salts Scrouge was revived once more but this time the circumstances were vastly different. He was in what seemed to be a small dark cave, very small in fact. So small that he and the spirit apparition thingy were shoved up right next to each other practically cheek by jowl. Not especially dignified for an elemental force capable of transporting mortal man through time and space, but Scrouge thought better of mentioning it. In any case the ghoul seemed to be really not in the mood for small talk.

'Right listen up,' it began. 'I am the ghost of Christmas Yet To Come...'

'You've told me that,' interjected Scrouge unhelpfully.

'Shut it!' snapped the ghost clearly beginning to lose his ethereal rag. For want of a quiet life Scrouge obeyed. 'Since you had such a flippin' marvellous childhood I've brought you into the future to show you your mortal remains!' This didn't sound too good and Scrouge felt the chill of fear returning. 'You are dead now and I'm going to show you your grave,' continued the spirit prosaically and then added, somewhat superfluously it seemed to Scrouge 'The general gist of this is that you need to realise that time is of the essence and we, I mean you and your accomplices need to chivvy it up a bit in the general area of working on the time machine project type thingy. In a nutshell you need to forget the whole "Let's take Christmas day off" malarkey and try and press on! Comprende?'

'Well that's all terribly specific,' spluttered Scrouge. 'I thought this was more of a general let-me-teach-you-something-deep-and-meaningful-about-life-and-Christmas-and-your-place-in-it kind of haunting?'

'No!' screamed the spirit hysterically. 'It's not that, it's what I just said... oh for crying out loud, let's just get on with it.' And with that it opened the door of the capsule and unceremoniously shoved Scrouge out. Still bleary from his second spell of unconsciousness Scrouge staggered out into what had most certainly once been a graveyard, but now looked an awful lot more like a battlefield. All around him across the churned up ground were soldiers and other uniformed militia. Some dead, some wounded and a few still actively engaged in full on warfare. A huge explosion suddenly tore a colossal chunk of dank earth from the ground and along with half a dozen or so miscellaneous body parts splattered it all over Scrouge and the, now emerging, dishevelled Santa Claus behind him. Scrouge was about to sink to his knees when a spritely figure in green combat smock, replete with several equipment belts, a helmet festooned with gadgets and toting a large hand gun of bizarre design grabbed them both and hauled them down behind a damaged, but still largely intact stone wall. Flashes of sinister light in satanic hues of red and yellow arced over their heads and screams could be heard echoing from the building opposite that was already encased in snarling licks of flame.

'Dear all that is holy!' breathed Scrouge shocked to his core, 'Remind me again what the point of this is?' This last he aimed at his spirit companion whom he turned to face only to find that in the force of the explosion the spirit's hood had been blown back and his goggles ripped roughly from his head. The net result of which meant that Scrouge could just about make out the features of his erstwhile assistant on his blood and grime smeared face. To literally cap it all the shock of white hair was unmistakable.

'Marley?' was all that Scrouge could force from his dry mouth before another figure jumped over the wall and practically landed on them, this one wearing a large black leather overcoat bristling with weapons, a wide brimmed hat jammed on his head.

'Who the chuffing hell are these two?' He snapped gruffly at the first figure, who turned out to be a woman with fiery blue eyes, wisps of short blonde hair and a rather fine chin prominent under her helmet and eyepieces.

'No idea,' shrugged the woman, 'but they're going to need a gun if they're going to be of any use to us.'

'Not sure they'd be of much use to us even then,' snarled the man. 'Landship is about to come up to the crossroads; this should be worth seeing. Time to give them a taste of their own sick alien medicine!'

With that he indicated the general direction of the event with a wave of a black gauntlet and then set about reloading one of his two large silver pistols.

The other three stared in the rough area he'd pointed to and sure enough a massive metal box with four giant caterpillar tracks one in each corner began to clank and belch its way around the corner alongside the graveyard. The so-called landship was covered in turrets with cannons and machine guns. Mighty diesel engines at the rear were doing a good job of creating an impromptu smoke screen as they coughed up great plumes of dense black smoke.

'Come on boys, give them something to chew on!' snarled the woman under her breath as she clenched her fist.

'Is that one on our side?' inquired Marley somewhat pathetically.

Before anyone could answer the gnarled man pointed to the left and growled: 'Tripod!' They all looked with horror as a monstrous three-legged machine nearly twice the size of the nearest building moved with almost impossible litheness and positioned itself at the far end of the road opposite the trundling, clanking tank.

'Let 'em have it boys!' yelled the woman and sure enough the metal fort let fly with every weapon it had. Cannons boomed, rockets launched and machine guns chattered away – to absolutely no effect whatsoever. Every shot went wide or simply pinged of the sleek saucer atop the three spindly legs.

'Oh dear,' muttered Scrouge and the others could do little more than agree silently. Then with an eerie whine the tripod began its response. A stem protruding from its saucer began to glow a ghastly green, and then yellow, and finally bright white and a single line of light shone out and flicked across the landship in a straight line from head to tail.

'Ha, is that all they've got!' declared Marley with rather premature sense of triumphalism as at first nothing appeared to happen. But then with a gut-churning screech two sides of the massive iron craft, which had been rather neatly sliced down the middle, began to fall away from each other. With two mighty crashes the halves of the vehicle thudded to earth sending dust, smoke and bits of the crew in every direction. As the great choking cloud engulfed them, Scrouge chose his moment to grab Marley and haul him desperately towards the time machine. More laser lights flickered around them as he heard the two soldiers behind them begin to lose off rounds. 'Behind you Fitch!' was the last words he heard as he bundled Marley into the capsule and, knowing now that they were in his very own invention, threw the switch that he himself had labelled "Home", with the intention that it would always take the travellers back to the present. He offered up a silent prayer that this future version of the machine worked as he'd always intended.

'I don't feel so good,' whispered Marley, but Scrouge barely heard him as the machine did its inhuman time-bending work around them.

Back in the laboratory Marley The More Inebriated had finished his splendid bottle of port and so was very glad when he heard the static sparking that heralded the return of the Time Machine. He was now somewhat the worse for drink and keen to return post-haste to his own time and continue celebrating, his revered position as the founder of time travel now, presumably, assured.

His spirits soared euphorically when he saw the wretched and bedraggled pair stumble from the still steaming glass capsule. Scrouge in particular looked shocked and defeated and no doubt was inclined to abandon his sense of seasonal cheer and return to work immediately. Marley The More Innocent's disposition was harder to discern as he was bundled swiftly from the room by Scrouge calling loudly for Mrs Bestial to attend.

The coast being pretty much clear, Marley The More Decrepit slipped out of the non-functioning time machine and into his own device. He closed the door firmly and then popped open a hidden panel beneath Scrouge's neatly etched "Home" switch. Inside which was another switch labelled somewhat less neatly, "Back To Future" – Marley The Most Ancient chuckled to himself and threw the switch. With this the time machine vanished somewhat less melodramatically than it had arrived, nice and neat, evidence removed, job done. Or so he thought.

Or perhaps he never did, as you shall see.

Back in the parlour, Scrouge had propped his fast-fading assistant up in the chair that he had earlier been warming with his own sleeping bulk. He peeled back the tattered remains of the Saint Nicolas outfit and discovered that Marley had been wounded rather badly by a stray shot in the melee they had barely escaped.

'My dear Marley, what has this all been about?' Scrouge asked in sympathetic tones as he removed the welding gauntlets he now recognised only too well and held Marley's hand in his own. All the colour had drained from Marley's face, but he still had a little strength left to lift his head up to his old master's gaze. His mouth moved dryly.

'You really don't want to know,' he began, 'but promise two small things to a dying man.' Scrouge realised the words were becoming a struggle so he leant closer and held Marley's hand a littler firmer.

'Speak my friend, I'm listening.'

'Forget about the time machine. It will bring no good to the world. Think of ways to fight the Martians that are surely returning, prepare mankind so that we can preserve our way of life. And even more than that, give me your word that you will always hold Christmas dear, we have to have something to make the fighting worthwhile.' And with that, and absolutely no regard as to how it affects the time line of the whole tale I've just relayed to you, Marley slipped away into the world beyond.

Scrouge agreed whole-heartedly with his sadly departed colleague, whose death it occurred to him was going to be rather hard to explain to the authorities. However there was no time to dwell on that as he really had to start work on something to change the world which currently seemed doomed to being wiped out perhaps only a score of years or so from today. It occurred to Scrouge at that moment that with all the time travelling he really had no idea what day it was. No clue could be discerned from the fire that had long since ebbed to silvery grey ashes.

Running to the window, he opened it, and put out his head.

'What's to-day?' cried Scrouge, calling downward to a boy in Sunday best clothes.

'Eh' returned the boy, with all his might of wonder.

'What's to-day, cloth ears?' said Scrouge growing a little impatient.

'To-day?' replied the boy. 'Why, Christmas Day.'

'It's Christmas Day.' said Scrouge to himself. 'I haven't missed it. The whole thing happened in a single night.' Not wanting to waste a moment he turned immediately and headed to his laboratory, diverting only to collect a bottle of claret and some fresh cheese from the pantry, to start dismantling his time machine and begin creating fearsome weapons of war.

'Sod you,' muttered the boy and shuffled off disconsolately.

And so our tale is ended in the mind-mangled fashion that only a time travelling story can elicit. And the moral of this story dear reader, should any such thing be required, is this: do not believe everything you read in stories. Merry Christmas, and god bless us all everyone.

V

An Aquanaut Misadventure

or Rocket Ship To The Bottom Of The Ocean!

The first view of Sir Grenville Lushthorpe's awesome invention appearing above the horizon was enough to take the breath away. As the lumbering Air Ministry airship made its inexorable way across the broiling East Ocean towards the rendezvous all the passengers found themselves elbowing for space at the forward observation window. An unseemly scrum ensued which dipped the airship nose alarmingly towards the waves below and forced the captain to ask them if they wouldn't mind awfully taking turns at the window. Thus chided the First Lord of the Admiralty Cuthbert pulled rank and took the first turn accompanied by Ellen Hall the waspish, newly-promoted Air Corps Captain replete with stiff new uniform.

Ellen squished her nose right up against the pane as she struggled to comprehend the massive construction growing ever larger in the gondola window.

'My word,' muttered the First Lord who was giving no sign of allowing anyone else to take a turn and had reduced the others to curious bobbing-around motions to try and see past his ample bulk.

Ahead of them in the glistening expanse of water was an incredible array of no less than twelve decommissioned dreadnought battleships arranged in two giant pontoons of six craft each. The majority of these hulks had had their superstructure removed (although the outer ones still retained their impressive 20 inch guns) and replaced with an enormous pair of wrought iron framework towers with gantries, cranes, elevators and service pipes running off the many levels. Suspended between these two lofty edifices was Lushthorpe's gob-smackingly massive Extra Deep Sea Rocket fully four hundred feet in height. At this distance the craft looked somewhat like gigantic stubby iron pencil, the pointy end dangling just above the choppy ocean waters. At its top, where the eraser would be so to speak, was a giant glass dome secured with hefty ironwork and penetrated in the middle by cluster of four giant chimneys. The middle sections were festooned with a variety of protrusions including rocket boosters, searchlights, harpoon guns, torpedo tubes, remote manipulation arms and airlocks; in fact everything one could imagine necessary for an extra-planetary mission. However this rocket was pointing firmly downwards rather than to the stars. In a nutshell she was, if you'll pardon the phrase, well tooled up.

Satisfied that all looked in order Cuthbert finally relinquished his spot at the window. We will draw a polite veil over the improper melee that ensued in a bid to replace him. Cuthbert was unaware of all this as, beckoning Ellen to join him, he sought out the inventor himself who was busying himself at a table covered with a motley assortment of charts and maps.

'Righty-ho Lushy,' boomed the First Lord, as was generally his way, 'I think it's about time we filled everyone in on what this junket is all about.' Lushthorpe conceded this with the barest of nods and Cuthbert instructed a nearby orderly to get the attention of his fellow travellers. Reluctantly, they dragged themselves away from the windows and formed a loose group. The reporters amongst them stood poised with notepads and pencils, there was even the pop of a powder flashgun as some eager beaver decided to record the moment.

'That's quite enough of that,' muttered Sir Grenville as he straightened up his lean figure ready to address the ensemble. He made quite a picture however as, clad in a white laboratory coat, he faced the room and all assembled could now see that was wearing large steel-framed optics that made his eyes appear several times larger than normal. He ran a bony hand through his thinning grey hair and cleared his throat melodramatically. With his other hand he pulled down the first of his large diagrams that was sprung on a coiling device in the ceiling. As he released the contraption it promptly sprang right back where it came from and two further attempts were necessary to finally get the scale drawing of the rocket to hold firm in its "down" position. This finally accomplished, he picked up an articulated pointing rod and gingerly tapped the diagram with some trepidation for fear it might re-coil itself once again. Relieved that this did not happen he finally felt ready to begin his briefing. 'My Lord, Ladies, gentlemen; and members of the press, welcome one and all to this inaugural launch of the Extra Deep Sea Rocket.' At this point he glanced around the room in a quite unnerving manner given the apparent size of his eyes and asked, somewhat prematurely, 'Any questions at this point?'

'Just bally get on with it!' snapped the First Lord whose veneer of rumbustious joviality was beginning to peel away as he steamed slightly in his full dress uniform.

'Um, right, yes indeed,' muttered Lushthorpe appearing slightly flustered now, he turned back to the chart and began indicating features with his stick in a seemingly entirely random sequence, 'Um the rocket, um observation deck. Err, harpoons, er no that's here...' More tapping '...retardation screws folded for lift off, er lift down, as it were, or, well whatever, you get the drift. Umm, airlocks, err remote manipulator arms?' he scanned the chart rapidly with his massive eyepieces, 'erm, no, can't quite locate that right now...'

'Enough!' bellowed the First Lord who now looked fit to explode. 'We get the picture, it's a whacking great underwater rocket, now step aside.' Before Lushthorpe could comply he shoved him out of the way and attempted to lower the second of the two diagrams. It in turn decided to copy its predecessor and reprise the whole uncoiling-re-coiling hoo-hah. Fortunately another helpful orderly stepped in rather sharpish to hold the chart down and prevent the First Lord spontaneously combusting. At this point Ellen was forced to stifle a laugh and a ripple of titters went round the room. The First Lord though was failing to see the funny side, 'Pull yourself together,' thundered Cuthbert, although it was somewhat unclear at whom this admonishment was aimed. Nevertheless it had the desired effect and the room settled down. The diagram the orderly was now clutching to prevent its untimely departure was rudimentary in composition. At the top, was a drawing of the rocket, directly below this a crude dotted line ran vertically downwards to where a drawing of a large ship lay on what was clearly intended to be the sea bed.

'As most of you are no doubt aware,' began the First Lord slowly regaining his composure, 'HMS Hesperus - a Ministry of Finance Fast Bullion Cruiser - recently disappeared in this very location with all hands lost. Now if that was not bad enough, and I must remind the ladies and gentlemen of the press that all information on this is currently embargoed, she was on a top secret mission at the time and carrying...' he paused melodramatically at this point, '...for reasons I cannot go into, fully one tenth of our gold bullion reserve.' A shocked gasp went round the room as the significance of this revelation began to sink in. At this point in proceedings the First Lord's attempts at severity where somewhat hampered by the airship inconveniently hitting a patch of turbulence. 'Yes quite, I cannot begin to tell you... oh *whoa there now*,' muttered the First Lord as the swaying of the airship sent one and all first one way and then the other. 'I cannot begin to, *lawky now, easy sailor*...' he continued as another burst of wobbling threatened to make him lose his footing. '*Woah, easy now, how's your father*...' He continued but the turbulence gave no indication of loosening its shaking grip on the ship. '*Right then, steady as she goes...* well we're going to go and... *whoopsie*, recover it with the... *lookout coming through*, rocket - briefing ended.' And with that he retired to his cabin to await the cessation of elemental hostilities, leaving the orderly to distribute the typed notes that were intended to accompany the briefing in a somewhat shambolic fashion.

Taking one of the sheets Ellen found a wicker chair near one of the airship's portholes and devoured its contents voraciously. As the Air Corps' youngest ever Flight Captain she had been handed the role of representing the Corps at the first launch of the mighty sea rocket. Truth be told there had been quite a childish squabble between the Air Corps and the navy as to who should have primary jurisdiction over the invention. The Air Corps were adamant that rockets were very much their province, however the Navy countered that since it was heading under the waves it had bugger all to do with a bunch of preening air jockeys. The Air Corps had not taken this too well, but a general reluctance on the part of any of the Wing Commanders to get their flying boots wet meant they huffed their way out of the running and let the fish-botherers get on with it. All this carry on had meant that no one from the Corps was very keen on having anything further to do with it, but nevertheless they felt they really ought to be represented, so the word went out for someone who might actually be up for such a jaunt. Ellen had jumped at the chance and her excitement grew further now as she read on. It seems that much mystery surrounded the loss of the Hesperus. There were rumours of conspiracies, and fevered speculation had led to a series of sea monster sightings by local fishermen and urchins and the like. There had even been some jittery talk of UFOs, but Ellen put it all down to over-eager imaginations.

What was indisputable though was how seriously the government was taking the loss of its ship. Fast Bullion Cruisers were not your common-or-garden steamship. Well-armed and armoured and faster than most in its class, one had never been lost before and the fact that this one had been stuffed to the gunnels with filthy lucre made it all the more galling. It occurred to Ellen, however, that the document in front of her was written in such a way that it seemed entirely plausible the government might actually claim the sinking was deliberate and merely a ruse to test out the Deep Sea Rocket. Assuming, of course, the mission was actually completed successfully. Time for further speculation was cut short as Ellen felt the bump that indicated that the airship was docked and it was time to meet the only real monster in this escapade – a preposterously huge under sea rocket!

They exited the door of the blimp onto the blustery gantry of one of the colossal wrought iron towers that supported the bulk of the rocket ship. Ellen had expected to emerge at the very top of the tower, but in fact the whole edifice was so monstrous that they were barely halfway up and would have to take an elevator to reach the summit. Needless to say they were still a fair old way up in the air and the wind was pretty brisk here. Ellen, Lushthorpe and Cuthbert (the only ones with clearance to actually enter the contraption) were forced to cling onto hats and railings alike. They made their way with some caution onto the gantry and the welcoming committee, which consisted of only two people, made their way equally cautiously to greet them. First of the two to reach them, dressed in a starched, white Homeland Navy uniform and cap (with essential chin strap deployed) introduced herself as Commodore Agnetha Freidkin - captain of the EDSe and also R. Freidkin was clearly of Scandinavian descent and looked a robust figure, not to be trifled with. Strong features and flamboyantly curly blonde hair made her also quite striking to look at. Salutes and handshakes were exchanged and attention then turned to the second of the two, a slightly weaselly looking figure in government issue grey trenchcoat, his ratty features made all the more stark by a pair of round spectacles that appeared slightly too small for his face.

'And who might you be?' enquired Cuthbert, sounding like he couldn't really care less, but he needed to know whether the man held a rank or not before offering a salute.

'Wrenish Snook,' replied the man in a dull and bored sounding voice, 'Ministry of Finance.'

'Oh a bean counter,' muttered Cuthbert, not quite under his breath. Before Snook could take offence however a large Bakelite speaker horn bolted to a nearby railing took this moment to announce 'TWELVE!' in quite unnecessarily loud tones. They all jumped, Snook included.

'Good lord what's that all about!' exclaimed Cuthbert quite taken aback. Lushthorpe stepped forward and began to usher the motley band towards a nearby elevator door, 'The countdown is well underway, I would suggest we make for the observation deck with all speed and I'll begin our tour once we are launched.' Without further ado they all did as they were told and the five of them crammed into a somewhat undersized lift car and began their cramped and rattly journey to the summit of the iron tower. During the ascent Snook broke the awkward silence, 'I had been expecting the Prime Minister to be in attendance, is he not amongst your company?'

'Ha,' laughed Cuthbert loudly, for indeed it was a bit of a sore point that the PM had decided to pull out at the last minute. Officially he had claimed "business of state", but Cuthbert speculated loudly, and somewhat wildly, that the truth was that the PM was probably scared of water. Or maybe he was just annoyed he didn't have a suitable uniform to wear (scandalously the PM had never served in the forces) – either way he'd cried off like a baby. It struck Ellen that despite an attempt at indifference Snook seemed somewhat dismayed by this response. Halfway up in the elevator they passed another large speaker horn that with impeccable timing announced 'ELEVEN!' They would have all jumped again had they not been too tightly packed in to move. 'Blasted thing,' spluttered Cuthbert to no one in particular.

By turns they eventually arrived at the top of the steel latticework tower and would have been relieved to be free of the cramped compartment had it not been for the dizzying visage that greeted them. Ahead, across several more gantries, was the impressive dome that topped the rocket. It comprised of large panes of curved glass held in place by strips of riveted metal and stood fully thirty feet high. Below this the titanic cylinder of the rocket dropped away right down to the ocean waves four hundred, or so, feet below. The entire edifice seemed alive with activity, be it technicians scurrying here or there, or vents belching steam, or pipes trickling waste fluids of one sort or another. To top it all the whole structure groaned and clanked in a quite unnerving way as it swayed to and fro in reaction to the stiff wind and the choppy waves below. Trying to take it all in Ellen marvelled at how such a massive structure could be held aloft like this at all, and could only be in awe of the effort that must have been involved in its construction. Conversely Cuthbert was making a beeline for the viewing dome where he fancied he could detect the aroma of a luncheon being prepared. Snook looked as if he couldn't care less about any of it and morosely brought up the rear as Lushthorpe and Freidkin led them finally off the rickety gantries and onto the rocket itself.

By this point the aggravatingly over-amplified announcements had boomed out TEN and NINE, oddly missed eight, and gone straight on to herald the arrival of SEVEN! Freidkin was now issuing commands with alacrity and aquanauts, in wonderfully ornate uniforms that seemed to be half "ahoy there sailor" and half "mission to the stars", scurried to comply. The great glass and bronze airlock was sealed behind them and, in the midst of all this frantic activity; the guests were ushered towards a suite of rather incongruous looking parlour furniture set up next to the massive central chimneys.

'You should all be able to observe proceedings from here. I would advise sitting down for launch itself, but subsequent to that we can take a walking tour of the rocket.' Informed Lushthorpe rubbing his hands with glee at the prospect of his mighty ship finally being unleashed.

'I wouldn't get yourself too lathered up Lushy old chap,' Cuthbert offered as he lowered his ample frame into an upholstered armchair, 'you are basically just sinking with style.' Ellen caught his wink and quickly, for Lushthorpe looked to have taken the comment none too well, tried her best to distract him as she also took her seat.

'What are these four chimneys for?' she enquired pouring on as much wide-eyed innocence as she could muster without giggling whilst patting one hand on the nearest of the great tubes. Lushthorpe eyed the First Lord through his magnifying eyepieces, but thought better of retorting in the end and turned to Ellen instead.

'Well now I was just coming on to that before I was so rudely interrupted. The first of the four chimneys is just that, a chimney, venting the fumes from the great steam turbines below us. Naturally this one will be capped just before diving to prevent the ingress of the ocean.' He paused for breath, spittle flecking his lips. 'The second and third tubes are what takes over to egress the smoke whilst submerged and is a cunning device of my own invention.'

'SIX!' blared out the overly eager countdown. Undisturbed by this Lushthorpe went on to explain how the two tubes held a complicated system of compressed bladders, rather like the air bags in an airship, that filled up with the smoke from the coal fired engines. When one was filled the system would, via an intricate series of cogs, pulleys and hatches, automatically switch to filling the other and the first one would be sealed and then released like a sort of balloon torpedo into the ocean to be recovered at the surface. The first tube would then be loaded with another empty gasbag ready to go when its turn came around again.

'Sounds somewhat overwrought to me,' sniped Snook tersely, causing the others to all look at him in surprise having quite forgotten he was even there.

'Jolly expensive more like,' guffawed the First Lord in a tone that would have happily graced the most bawdy of pantomimes. In very slightly more serious tone he enquired of Lushthorpe 'What's the fourth one for then?'

'Oh that,' replied the professor wistfully, 'that's just to make it look symmetrical.'

Before any of them could consider this further the bustle of the aquanauts attending dials, levers and other assorted workstations rose to a new level and the vociferous announcements barked out again, 'FIVE! FOUR! THREE!'

'Oh my word,' exclaimed Ellen with a mixture of giddy excitement and outright cold fear gripping the arms of her chair tightly. All others not required to stand for the launch moved with great alacrity to park their posteriors.

'TWO!'

'Lordy,' squeaked the First Lord with some angst as, with a great cascade of smoke and sharp tongues of flame, the rocket boosters strapped just below the dome burst into life. It was as if a ring of giant roman candles surrounded the entire deck had just been lit showering great plumes of sparks down onto the dome above them. The great rocket could be felt pulling hard against its restraints as it strained to plunge into the ocean.

'ONE!'

There was the briefest of pauses and then, 'LIFT OFF!' bellowed the announcement, somewhat incorrectly. Thus commanded the rocket was duly released and with an unearthly moan the entire craft began to plunge sickeningly downwards like the enormous iron bullet it was. One and all felt their stomachs lurch violently upwards and a tremendous shudder shook them as the rocket hit the ocean and but continued to plummet unabated.

Ellen found herself unable to restrain a whoop of sheer delight; their epic adventure to the seabed had begun.

The descent to the seabed was an amazing series of events. First the gantries flashed by in a shower of flames and smoke and then the ocean itself, at first with a watery magical light and then increasingly dark as the rockets were extinguished by the briny waters. Finally nothing could be seen beyond the dome save what could be picked out rushing past in the gloomy light emitting from the few deck lamps alone (which was mostly a few startled fish). At this point our protagonist's stomachs having acclimatized somewhat to the relentless drop, Lushthorpe offered to show them around. Tentatively, as the craft was still shaking spasmodically, Cuthbert, Ellen, Freidkin and Snook all followed the inventor through an airlock in the floor, which was sealed behind them, and down an ornate spiral staircase into the staterooms below. These were indeed very well appointed with cabins for all, should they be required, a smoking room, washrooms, kitchens and, much to Cuthbert's delight, a banqueting hall where a splendidly smelling repast was being laid out as they wandered through.

'Of course the whole ship is fully pressurized so you should experience no discomfort,' lectured Lushthorpe with extravagant hand gestures as he led them down through another airlock onto a more industrial looking level festooned with pipes, coils of rope and other miscellaneous sub-nautical looking equipment. Before showing them round he called them over to a handle on the wall painted red and adorned with a large gaudy sign which read "UNDER NO CIRCUMSTANCES PULL THIS LEVER!" and a smaller one underneath that read somewhat less bombastically "Except in extreme emergency."

'Now, of course, you may be wondering what should be done in the unlikely event of an emergency during our journey to the cold depths of the bleak ocean floor,' began Lushthorpe.

'Well I wasn't,' interrupted Cuthbert, 'but I bally well am now!'

'Relax my lord,' countered Lushthorpe, 'in such circumstances I need only depress this lever that you will observe here. A warning will sound and the crew will begin their evacuation procedures in their own personal diving suits. Meanwhile we will return to the staterooms where, once all airlocks are secured, I can pull a second lever and the dome and attendant levels will detach and float safely back to the surface.'

At this point Snook surprised them all by piping up again in his squeaky mouse voice, 'This second handle, where is that precisely?' Delighted that someone was actually taking an interest in his contraption Lushthorpe replied at great length and Snook proceeded to take notes in a tiny notebook with a miniscule, but perfectly formed pencil, which resembled something a child might use; a creepy, rat-faced child.

While this was happening Captain Freidkin took the opportunity to show the others some of the features of this level.

'We are fully equipped to either defend the rocket or carry out recovery operations as required,' she explained in sonorous tones somewhat more easy on the ear than Lushthorpe's slightly nasal whine. She guided them carefully between wooden cases and reels of steel cable to where one of the harpoon guns was positioned in the wall next to a large round porthole, through which could be seen only utter darkness. The harpoon gun itself was an amazing contraption mounted in a swivelling mechanism in the wall so it could be aimed from within with the aid of a large arc light, currently unlit, mounted atop the firing mechanism. An elaborate, apparently steam-powered, winching box with tiny brass winding handle on the side sat underneath.

The harpoon has five hundred yards of high strength lightweight cable, and the recovery mechanism is power-assisted from the coal turbines. The arc light is extremely powerful, capable of illuminating easily a hundred...' Before she could finish her sentence the on-board announcements crackled into life again and apropos of entirely nothing loudly declared "EIGHT!" They all, with the exception of Snook, looked at each other bemused. Then an even greater shuddering than normal took place and it was evident that their descent seemed to be slowing. An industrial sounding screeching noise could also be heard coming from somewhere many floors below them. Freidkin was nonplussed, 'It sounds as though the propellers have been reversed and the landing legs are being lowered, we must be approaching the sea bed.' There was another great rumble and the whole ship rocked again, causing the First Lord to finally lose his footing and crash into the harpoon. In doing so he must have triggered some sort of switch as the harpoon lamp sparked into life illuminating the sea outside. Ellen gasped as she followed this beam of light and realized she was staring into the great looming eyes of what appeared to be an eight-limbed sea monster of gigantic proportions, which was descending alongside them in the gloom. She rushed to the porthole as the thing seemed startled by being suddenly thrust into the spotlight and proceeded to retreat rapidly from view.

'Monster! There!' was all Ellen could muster as Lushthorpe and a recovering Cuthbert joined her and Freidkin to squint out of the portholes trying to make out the rapidly disappearing many-limbed shape in the murky waters.

'Nearly gone!' bellowed Cuthbert in frustration, but Ellen was determined not to let it escape. As quick as you like she took hold of the harpoon gun and aimed its great brass mechanism at the last spot where she fancied the monster had been and fired. With a loud crack, the harpoon shot off into the water along the light beam with its cable taut behind it. With bated breath they all watched it disappear from sight so only the glinting line of the cable was visible. As they stared the line finally went slack and then taut again and showed no signs of falling away or drifting.

'By George,' exclaimed Cuthbert, 'I think you've hit it! Reel her in girl, reel her in!'

Needing no second invitation Ellen grabbed the ridiculously tiny brass wheel on the winch mechanism and amidst great venting of steam from the side of the contraption began to whizz it around in almost comical fashion.

At first naught appeared to happen, but the cable was still taut and the motors were straining audibly. Nothing was yet visible in the harpoon light beam when suddenly, despite Ellen's frantic winding, the rope slacked off and then an ominous black shape could be seen moving towards them. They all stared slack-jawed as the blob grew limbs and eyes and a great swollen head. It was around about this time that it began to dawn on them that they were no longer controlling its arrival and the monster was in fact racing headlong towards them.

'Whoa there sailor!' exclaimed the First Lord.

'Bracing positions!' added Freidkin, rather more helpfully. But it was too late for any of that, the monstrous shape was upon them almost immediately, blotting out the view from the porthole and then crashing with a mighty, and suspiciously metallic sounding, clang into the rocket and causing it to judder violently throwing them all to the floor. The lights flickered, then cut out and they were briefly in darkness before emergency illumination lit up the whole floor in an eerie red glow. The noise of a baleful klaxon resounded from somewhere in the floors below.

'Lawks,' babbled Ellen, finding her feet first and hauling herself up to look out at the shape of the creature now floating a few feet from the rocket, 'that's not a sea monster, it's some sort of submersible craft.' As if to prove her point the two discs she had taken for eyes suddenly became bright lights shining directly at them causing them all to turn away from the porthole shielding their eyes.

'Quite so, quite so,' came a snide, and extremely boring, voice from the far side of the room and they all looked round to see Snook standing next to the now depressed emergency lever. In his hand was a tiny, brass, five-barrelled pistol, clearly cocked and ready to fire.

'Stay where you are, I have one bullet for each of you, and I am a perfectly respectable shot.'

'Good lord Snape what are you playing at!' growled the First Lord.

'It's Snook you imbecile, and what I'm playing at is destroying your deep sea rocket and depriving the homeland of both its head of the Navy and chief scientist.'

'Well I'll be damned Snark, you'll hang for this!'

'Snook! It's Snook!' said Snook tetchily, 'now be quiet unless you want me to put a hole through the middle of your forehead.' He waggled the pistol and this time no one dared offer any further threats. 'That's better. Of course I already have all the gold from the wreck of the Hesperus and once all of the crew have completed their well-drilled, and perhaps overly obedient, evacuation I shall be on my way, leaving you to meet your end as you see fit.' Rather deflated by this, Cuthbert sat himself down forlornly on a nearby crate and before Ellen or Freidkin could hatch any cunning plans the loudspeakers crackled into life again 'EVACUATION COMPLETE!' they ranted. Snook glanced down at the twin dials of his chronograph.

'Forty eight seconds precisely and the well-drilled imperial rats have abandoned their sinking vessel. This has all been too easy, in your arrogance you all took me for some chinless accountant and didn't even bother to check my credentials.' He started to make his way to the spiral staircase. 'I must say it's a shame your cowardly Prime Minister felt unable to join us that would have been the creamy icing on a rather delicious cake.'

'But who the blazes are you, and what do you want?' spluttered Lushthorpe his eyes, wild and bloodshot through his magnifying lenses, giving him an almost ogreish look in the flickering red light. By this time Snook was almost at the airlock and he had to backtrack slightly and bend down to reply, in a less than dignified position for his lanky frame.

'Eh what's that? Oh, who are we? Oh right, probably should have mentioned that. We are the Fourth Day Ascension League and you will he hearing from us.' And with that he disappeared through the airlock slamming it shut behind him. Freidkin immediately leapt up and mounted the stairs to try the hatch.

'Locked I'm afraid,' she announced tersely to general sounds of disheartenment.

'Is there any other way out Lushthorpe?' enquired the First Lord. The inventor was slouched head in hands, which Cuthbert took to be not altogether encouraging.

'None whatsoever I'm afraid, below us are only the engine rooms, stores and crew levels and the crew themselves are all gone.' He shook his head disconsolately. 'And to think that I gave him full directions on how to detach the dome and escape,' he wailed to himself in a slightly odd feline way, which was then accompanied by a judder and a series of popping sounds from above their heads. 'There he goes now,' he wailed some more.

'The monster is on the move,' alerted Ellen moving the harpoon light to track its progress as it ascended up the side of the rocket. Those that were interested craned their heads at various portholes as the octo-machine disappeared from view and then its headlight-eyes heralded its return, this time dragging the giant dome of the rocket behind it. Standing serenely next to one of the windows they could just about make out what they took to be Snook looking back at them. He half raised his arm as if to wave, but then thought better of it and let it drop again.

They all sat in the eerie red gloom for a few minutes desperately thinking of any plan that might allow them to escape. The only sounds were the distant klaxon that still wailed somewhere below them and the continuing rumble of the steam engines. For want of something better to do Ellen began opening store boxes, so far she'd found only overalls and tins of out-of-date pilchards.

'He didn't even leave us any lunch,' moaned the First Lord to himself not really getting into the spirit of trying to escape, and then added somewhat pessimistically, 'We are completely and utterly doomed,' accompanied by a forlorn and overly melodramatic sigh. Trying her best to ignore him another thought occurred to Ellen as she and Freidkin prized open a further crate, this time of heavy weave fisherman's sweaters.

'The engines are still running, can't we just power ourselves to the surface?'

'Alas the controls were all in the dome, bit of a design-flaw I would say,' replied Freidkin somewhat sarcastically as she made her way around the giant chimneys in the centre of the floor to look for something more useful to them.

'Wonderful,' sighed Ellen. She opened another crate and pulled out what appeared to be some sort of breathing apparatus. 'How about this?' she asked holding one up for Lushthorpe to take a look, 'there's enough for us all.'

'It's a gasmask my dear, in case of fumes and such like...' His voice tailed off as a rumble shook one of the giant chimneys followed by a hair-raising squeak much like a giant balloon being twisted, which started loudly and then faded away above their heads.

'Oh for the sake of all that is holy, whatever now?' moaned the First Lord clenching his teeth and pulling a face that resembled a stroppy toddler. As if on cue, his tummy chose this moment to rumble loudly in sympathy.

'That was the... oh wait a minute,' Lushthorpe stood up abruptly, 'I think I might have a way to get us out of here... Ellen we need your gasmasks after all, and we'll need lifejackets, flares, a penknife...' Heartened by this sudden turn of events Ellen and the Captain began to look through the rest of the stores with renewed energy. Even Cuthbert pulled himself to his feet in order to be of some assistance.

'Good man Lushy, I knew we'd be fine. What's this plan of yours then?'

'Oh you're not going to like it,' muttered Lushthorpe, 'you're not going to like it at all.'

By now it was late afternoon and a warm Spring sun was casting its benevolent rays down onto the now quieter waters of the great East Ocean. A herring gull had landed and was bobbing thoughtfully in the swelling tide, contemplating whether to try for more fish or fly on for dry land. Not far away the great dreadnought pontoons with their now empty superstructures were swaying gently on the ocean swells. Alerted by the evacuated aquanauts, who had begun floating to the surface only minutes before; rescue crews were now putting out in all directions looking for signs of the dome returning to the surface. The bird looked down into the water and thought it saw a fish some way below. Its small brain did some basic trigonometry and reasoned that given its depth perhaps it wasn't a fish, but rather something bigger and further away. Oh good, it contemplated, a dolphin or perhaps a whale. How nice, it mused, although it is rather rushing towards me now. Then without so much as a "by your leave" the giant shape broke the surface scattering fish and gulls in all directions. It was an enormous grey balloon, fully thirty yards long and two wide that stood on end for a moment and then crashed down onto the ocean surface. It floated there for a second or two before suddenly bursting in a great cloud of acrid grey smoke like some giant's rubbish magic trick. As the smoke cleared four motley figures wearing gasmasks and lifejackets could be seen bobbing in the water flailing their arms to dispel the smoke. One of them reached a hand up and released a yellow flare, which arced through the air past the now hovering gull. Bloody whale, it thought, now it's shooting at me. He defecated in its general direction and made off for somewhere more peaceful.

Below him the bedraggled heads bobbed in the swell - having made good their escape by somehow managing to crawl into Lushthorpe's ridiculously over-engineered exhaust gas balloon expulsion system and allowing themselves to be thus duly expulsed. Spotting the flare a rescue boat turned and headed towards them and ripping off his gasmask the First Lord managed a throaty, 'Ahoy sailor!' that finally seemed the appropriate thing to say. Ellen was keeping her thoughts to herself as she also removed her mask and took in large gasps of fresh salty air, but somehow, she reflected, it was unlikely they had heard the last of Wrenish Snook and his Fourth Day Ascension League.

And truth be told, dear reader, they really had no idea of just what calamities were yet to befall them, no idea at all.

Not one clue. None.

VI

Lost In The Great White

'Well that's a very rum do,' muttered the PM as he, the Homeland Defence (and Attack) Secretary – The Right Honourable Arthur Coward - and the King's Butler – Ms Chuffingwell-Happy stood and stared through a three foot round hole in the ceiling of the King's favourite bedchamber and out to the blue sky and lazily drifting clouds beyond.

They continued to stare for a moment or two longer before the PM, who felt somewhat uncomfortable amongst so much regal finery (scandalously the PM was a republican), could think of nothing better to add than 'Very rum indeed.' Somewhat baffled he finally turned his gaze from the gaping aperture to survey the scene of rubble, sawdust and general disarray that lay around them. 'And you say that the King was, um, removed through this very chasm last night?' Coward nodded sheepishly and continued to stare at the hole lest he catch the PM's eye. Ms Chuffingwell-Happy formed a barely discernable scowl and tut-tutted very disapprovingly. 'Well in all my days I'm not sure I've ever beheld anything quite so rum. When did you say your man, the admiral, was getting here to look into all of this?'

'Er, man?' coughed Coward under his breath, 'not sure I ever mentioned anything about a man.'

Before the PM could interrogate him further on the subject there was a jovial rap on the well up-holstered oak door and a rotund and equally jovial looking police constable entered with a cheery 'What ho all!' It was a day when the PM's demeanour was to be in a constant state of being taken aback and he was beginning to get a little bored of it.

'Admiral Sherman?' enquired the PM, extremely sceptically.

'Oh no ho ho,' laughed the constable his cheeks glowing rosier by the minute, 'I'm not the admiral oh deary me no.' Nothing much was going to surprise the PM now, but before he could so much as utter a "who the devil is then", there was snuffling around the door and what appeared to be a large sheepdog-wolf cross with a shaggy brown coat and a very smart blue waistcoat, replete with gold Metropolis Police badge, bustled into the room and began some earnest sniffing amongst the dusty trappings of the bedroom.

'That's the Admiral dear boy', beamed the policeman and duly plonked himself down on the King's very bed. At the sound of her name, the dog paused briefly and raised one hairy eyebrow at the PM, before continuing to sniff excitedly. The PM glared accusingly at his Secretary, 'I do hope this is some sort of joke Coward! That's not a detective, that's a blinkin' mutt!' Before Coward could even begin to formulate the first syllable of his reply the dog turned and snarled angrily, not insubstantial teeth bared, at the PM who went quite white around the gills.

'Oh I wouldn't call her that if I were you,' chortled the constable quite beside himself with mirth, 'She prefers Admiral Sherman, or Regina to her friends.'

'Er good dog... er Admiral,' squeaked the PM, and somewhat placated the dog resumed her sniffing, moving now towards the fireplace. The Defence Secretary suddenly found his voice as Chuffingwell-Happy continued to scowl in such a way as to suggest she was very unimpressed with the whole carry on, 'I know it's a little queer, but the Admiral is the best operative we have. She'll get to the bottom of this and no mistake.'

'Well I blasted well hope so,' muttered the PM looking around for somewhere not too dusty to park his posterior. Finally spying a reasonably sturdy looking chair he duly sat, 'tell me one thing constable, why is she called The Admiral?'

'Her idea that,' guffawed the constable. 'Seems they aren't too keen on giving ranks to animals in the constabulary even though she's our most decorated operator. So she renamed herself Admiral so she outranks us all, oh it does make me laugh!' With this the constable proceeded do exactly that with great bellowing guffaws, which caused the Defence Secretary to stifle a chortle under his breath. Even the PM was finding it a little hard not to chuckle, Ms C-H however could not have looked any sterner.

'Right, right,' offered the PM raising an arm to instil some calm on the situation. 'Ms Chuffingwell, I think perhaps tea and biccies for everyone and for the benefit of...' he glanced at the dog still busy at her snuffling investigations, 'er, The Admiral, perhaps you could just recap on our understanding of events to date.' This last was aimed at the Defence Secretary who duly obliged as Ms C-H, still looking distinctly not best pleased with the situation, spoke into an electric speaking tube near the bed to order the aforementioned refreshments.

Taking a place centre stage the Secretary began to recount the tale of how the butler had knocked thrice on the royal bedchamber door this very morning before deciding it best to arouse the king from his slumbers, only to find a deficit of kings and a surfeit of clodding great holes in the ceiling. The only conclusion offering itself was that one had been removed through t'other, but the whys and wherefores of the situation were yet to be ascertained with any degree of clarity or, indeed, at all. With this final pronouncement Admiral the dog was heard to tut and shake her head slightly. Before the PM could venture his tuppence ha'penny on the subject a train's whistle followed by a whirring and clanking sound interrupted their flow. Then on a hitherto unnoticed miniature railway track that entered from a hole in the wall appeared a tiny steam-powered locomotive towing behind it a tender stacked with bourbons and four cups of steaming beverage in white porcelain train carriage shaped cups. 'Well I never,' muttered the PM rubbing his hands at the thought of a decent brew. However a loud bark from The Admiral brought him back to the present with a start.

'Oh ho ho ho ho, what have we here?' bellowed the, still as yet unintroduced constable, jumping up with a spritely manner that belied his size and moving to the middle of the room where The Admiral was tapping urgently with one paw. As all looked on, and the PM gave only half a glance to his now cooling cup of tea, the constable knelt down and delicately pulled a small white flower from amongst the scattered debris. 'Well all my days, what have you found here girl?' Admiral sat herself down on her haunches looking really rather pleased with herself, if such a thing were possible in a hound.

'If I may?' ventured the Defence (and Attack) Secretary reaching for his spectacles, 'I'm no great expert, but I do consider myself something of an amateur horticulturist.' He studied the flower carefully as Ms C-H finally distributed the cups of tea, including pouring one into a bowl produce by the constable that The Admiral lapped at noisily.

'Well I do believe it's a Lesser Spotted Diamond Edelweiss,' offered the Secretary and with this The Admiral paused slurping briefly and appeared somewhat impressed at the diagnosis. 'And this is certainly a great breakthrough for us as these flowers are only found in one part of the world!' All looked on expectantly, however despite taking a large inward breath in anticipation of a great pronouncement it gradually became apparent that the secretary was perhaps struggling to recall the exact origin of the specimen.

'And that would be?' enquired the PM, hoping to chivvy things along as the Secretary was starting to turn puce. Finally to the relief of all he exhaled uttering breathlessly 'The Crested Mountains!' He seemed very pleased with himself, however this did not go down so well with The Admiral who buried her head in her paws. The constable who was looking only to the dog's reaction chipped in, 'Not sure The Admiral is with you on that your holiness, care to have another stab?'

'Eh, what, really?' muttered the Secretary, quite taken aback, mostly at having being caught out with a rather wild guess. 'Er, no perhaps not, then maybe the Gaulish Riviera?' he offered, but this was greeted only with more head burying and an impatient growl from the hound.

'Not there your worshipfulness, have another crack,' chuckled the constable.

'What, really? Oh, I don't know,' he looked to the PM for help, but help there came none as the PM concentrated on his cuppa. 'The Cloud Island then?' tried the Secretary one more time and was relieved to see that Admiral nodded her head and returned noisily to her bowl of tea.

'Splendid work all,' said the PM sounding really rather amused with proceedings. 'Then we have to start our investigations there by all accounts'. A nod of approval to Admiral was followed by an inquisitive look at the Secretary, 'Cloud island, that's one of the colonies isn't it? Who's our chap on the ground there?'

'Well now,' began the Secretary relieved to be returning to an area where his knowledge was such he was unlikely to be overruled by a dog, 'It was Caruthers-Simpleton, but we've not heard a peep from him in yonks. Jungle drums are hinting that he may have gone native.'

'The plot thickens,' muttered the PM. 'I assume we've already taken action?'

'Indeed, indeed, a gunboat has been despatched, but it's had to wait for the southern approaches to thaw before it can get anywhere near the capital.'

'Inconvenient,' summed up the PM. 'Then we must have an agent or two in the area?'

'Two of our best were alerted by rocket-propelled pigeon only last week.'

'Then they are the only game in town. Be so good as to fire off another pigeon or two and let's see where that gets us.'

'It will be done forthwith,' and with that Coward drained his tea and set forth. The PM and The Admiral raised an eyebrow at each other in mutual recognition that this case was a long way from being solved. Nevertheless the PM was moved to mutter a 'Good girl,' under his breath, raising his carriage shaped cup in a simple salute to the hound. 'Jolly well done.'

About a week later, Caruthers-Simpleton rolled over on his side and gazed drunkenly out through the large window at the bottom of his cabin wall across the strange, eerily lit land that was currently his pied-a-terre. He took a deep suck on his hot fermented millet drink through its bamboo straw, idly played with his pencil moustache and chuckled to himself at how cushy his number had become. Ever since that creepy Snook chap had arrived and offered him twice his normal civil service salary to cut communications with those pompous twits in the Metropolis, whilst simultaneously turning a blind eye to the comings and indeed goings on the north side of the island his prospects had improved immensely. At some point there was almost certain to be a great reckoning, but with the southern passages currently frozen solid that time was some way off arriving. Cloud

Island was certainly a weird and wonderful place to be marooned. In point of fact it was actually an old, hopefully dormant, volcano with a large flat top that was surrounded six months of the year by ice and had some peculiar cloud formations that gave it both its name, and its peculiar ambience. The most common of these events was a thick low cloud that would drift across the top of the mountain about four feet off the ground. This would have the curious effect of hiding everyone's heads as they carried out their business and had encouraged the locals to build windows at ground level to allow them to at least observe the headless bodies scurrying this way and that. It was through one of these low-level apertures that Caruthers-Simpleton now gazed out from his bedroll at the rather fetching lower reaches of a pleasingly buxom milkmaid, in a low cut peasant dress, now striding her way approximately in his direction. A wooden yoke across her barely visible shoulders carrying a splashing milk pail on a rope on either side caught his attention also. It was nearly midday and perhaps a cool drink of milk, and who knew what else this lovely two thirds of a woman might be prepared to offer him might be just the ticket. He pushed open the wooden framed window and called out in a somewhat slurry voice,

'Well hello my good lady, can you spare me a glass of your fresh milk?' the woman, turned without hesitation and strode purposefully, and somewhat robustly, in his direction.

'My pleasure, good sir,' came a rather gruff and low sounding voice, not entirely what he was expecting, but she seemed keen enough. He loosened the cord of his dressing gown (as he was yet to make it from his bedroll this morning) and allowed it so slip open just a little. Despite the fact the he had gone considerably to seed in his three years on the Island, Simpleton still considered himself quite a catch in a land of hard-toiling peasant farmers.

'Come to the door and I'll give you something for your trouble.'

Too right I will, thought the island governor to himself as he kicked open the rickety wooden door with his foot. A little of the island's low cloud drifted into the room as the bulky form of the woman approached. I wonder what this delightful apparition looks like, wondered Simpleton to himself. Doesn't really matter too much after two millet beers, he mused slurping up the last dregs. With great anticipation he stretched himself out on the yak fur coverings whilst the woman made her way around the side and her body, somewhat larger than expected, suddenly filled the doorway, yolk, milk pails and all. Head, as yet, still not visible.

'Come in dear so I might gaze upon your visage,' entreated Simpleton feeling really rather drunk. He gazed up and gave a gasp of horror as through the swirling whiteness at the top of the door came first a large brass pistol barrel followed, in timely fashion, by the burly arms and grizzled face of a rather large man wearing a broad rimmed black hat. The rest of the outfit turned out to be a rather well crafted disguise, replete with fake arms attached to the pails, and an entirely false bosom over which the arms and grizzled features of Tobias Fitch now loomed down towards the cowering Simpleton; who was now trying desperately to pull his barely adequate dressing gown around his otherwise naked body.

'Got you, you little rat!' growled Fitch jabbing the pistol towards him as he crashed into the hut looking faintly ridiculous in his two-thirds of a milkmaid disguise. 'Eeek,' was all that Simpleton could offer in reply. Fitch began to peel off the bizarre costume with one burly arm, whilst all the while keeping his large revolver pointed at Simpleton's nose. After a brief struggle the outfit was off and Fitch stood in all his glory dressed in a long black coat that had been hidden underneath, the only odd thing being that the bottom half of his legs were still in character, as it were, resplendent in thick tights and peasant girl fur bootees.

'Don't suppose you know anything about the disappearance of the King's person now, do you?'

'I might be able to help you with that,' droned a curiously monotonous voice that emanated from the rat-like features of a rather creepy looking man who had appeared silently from behind a partition at the rear of the hut. Fitch scowled but did not move as he noticed the malevolent figure had a small, but lethal enough looking five-barrelled pistol trained between his eyes. Fitch cursed himself inwardly for not having been more on the ball, but he'd been so concerned with getting the drop on Simpleton that he'd forgotten to look out for accomplices. He continued to train his own gun on the cowering man, while he kept his eyes fixed on the newcomer.

'And who might you be when you're at home?' growled Fitch with barely disguised annoyance.

'Snook,' drawled Snook in really the most boring sounding tones Fitch had ever had the misfortune to clap ears upon. 'Wrenish Snook is the name and you are somewhat earlier than I would have thought possible. But never mind, I have your king billy-boy incarcerated nearby.' With those words and not a syllable more Snook then ducked back behind the partition. With the barest flicker of movement Fitch adjusted his pistol and fired three horrifically loud shots at the general area where Snook should have been, blasting great holes in the bamboo and reed screen and filling the little hut with acrid smoke.

'Too slow,' came the familiar dull tones from *behind* Fitch and he felt the cold metal of the pistol pushed into his neck. 'Be so kind as to drop your weapon,' drawled Snook. Fitch had no option but to comply, though his brain was now churning on how this rodent-like creature been able to move so swiftly. Maybe the thin mountain air was getting to him.

'Make yourself useful, governor, and disarm this gentleman,' sneered Snook in the vague direction of Caruthers-Simpleton who shivering in his barely adequate dressing gown, but having been sobered up considerably by the goings-on, shuffled to comply.

Some five minutes later with Fitch relieved of his coat and hat, and with a small pile of weapons including pistols, knives, blowpipes and other paraphernalia crudely piled in the middle of the room the disarming was deemed to have been, probably, completed. In any case time was getting on and, with barely a nod to the pathetic form of the governor, Snook beckoned that Fitch should move outside into the low cloud. And so the two odd headless figures made their way across the village, Fitch now in only his undershirt and shorts, milkmaid's tights and bootees, Snook in his dull grey trenchcoat and equally uninteresting grey shoes, brass pistol to the fore urging his prisoner onwards.

After a few minutes trudging, the gravel path gave way to a crude rope bridge and Fitch made his way somewhat uneasily onto this contraption. The whole affair was shaking and wobbling so much that Fitch nearly lost his footing once or twice. It soon became apparent that although one side of the bridge was secured on the mountain the other was attached to something a lot less stable. Fitch's suspicions were confirmed as the bridge finally lead on to a wooden and iron gangway that appeared to stretch off into the clouds with a large canvas envelope bobbing gently either side of them. It was most likely they were now on the top surface of a colossal airship-type contraption, moored in the clouds alongside the cliff face. Truly it was so big that Fitch could not make out the extent of it in any direction, as it's off-white bulk merged into the low cloud billowing all around them. Here and there similar gangways stretched out at right angles to their pathway and the occasional vent or mechanical artefact could be glimpsed, but nothing made a sound and Fitch could only guess at their utility. A few steps further and Fitch began to make out another figure in grey standing near a dark hatch in the superstructure. As he got closer he realised that the verminous features looked rather familiar and he could no longer hear footsteps on the planks behind him. With horror he realised that Snook was no longer behind him, but standing, pistol in hand, in front of him gesturing languidly for Fitch to descend into the body of the airship. Fitch's brain could hardly begin to surmise how Snook was managing his mysterious vanishing tricks before he was forced to descend an iron ladder into the ship. The heavy hatch was slammed shut and many bolts were thrown, leading Fitch to immediately discard any thoughts of making good an escape that way. Instead he continued to descend until his foot failed to find a rung at the bottom of the ladder and he realised it had terminated above a simple hole in the canvas, below which was who knew what?

'Hello below!' he called out, as much to see if his voice echoed back off any solid surface, but was surprised instead to hear a reply.

'Wot ho old thing,' came the unmistakably chirpy tones of King William the eleventh of that name. Without hesitation Fitch let go of the ladder and dropped rapidly into the light below. To his great relief he hit relatively soft airship canvas after a drop of only ten feet or so. Taking in his surroundings Fitch found himself in a room that was canvas on all sides but two. Ahead of him through narrow iron bars was the rather bizarre visage of the King of New Albion still in his monogrammed pyjamas, nightgown and nightcap, sitting cross-legged on the gently bobbing floor grinning from ear to ear. 'Wot ho old thing,' chirped King Billy the eleventh again, 'Looking for me by any chance?' Before Fitch could offer anything in return, the king cryptically put his finger to his lips and then pointed over Fitch's shoulder. Finding his feet slowly on the floor which was about as steady as a trampoline isn't, Fitch slowly rotated about himself to look towards the other side of the canvas room where, with a slight start, he realised another, smaller, figure was sitting looking at him inscrutably. This person turned out to be a young, nimble looking woman of vaguely oriental appearance. Black hair neatly pulled back in a ponytail, she was clad in an impressive royal blue eastern-style jacket and black acrobat's leggings and pumps. She tipped her head slightly in greeting but said nothing. Her muscular but calm demeanour suggested some sort of training, and Fitch assumed she must be another agent, perhaps from the Sino-Chinese Empire. Not an ally as such but perhaps not an enemy either. Since it was unlikely she spoke any English, he tipped a salute instead. The woman gave a slight frown and then with two fingers of one hand pointed first to her eyes and then to Fitch's somewhat unsteady legs. He glanced down, and only then remembered the milkmaid disguise still adorning his lower half. He couldn't immediately think of the international sign language for "it's a long story" so he just shrugged in the most non-committal way he could muster. Before further wordless confusion could be engaged in there came a juddering in the airship and without warning the canvas floor gave way and Fitch and the woman were both sent tumbling into a narrow fabric tunnel.

'Cheerio then old fruits,' offered the King by way of goodbye.

Since he was tumbling headfirst, Fitch was first relieved that the tube was not very long, but then pretty much immediately annoyed-as-buggery that the fall was terminated by him cracking his head on a hard iron disk. He barely had time to mutter half an oath before the woman landed on him with a thump and then the floor began to descend and they were both forced to hold on to a cold iron pipe which was all there was between them, the elements and an drop of unknown depth below them. The apparatus to which they were both now desperately clinging was in fact a pair of three-foot wide iron disks connected by a six-inch diameter solid metal pipe. Above that unseen cables and pulleys were dropping them rapidly to the surface where they suddenly stopped with an unseemly thump, tossing them both out onto unyielding ice.

Fitch rubbed his sore head and waited as the swirling stars slowly gave way to the sheer whiteness of their surroundings. In every direction he could make out only white fog or ice with not a feature to be seen with the exception of the oriental lady and the great contraption they had descended on. This now turned out to be a great, iron toothed circular drill, above which was the pipe they had held on to and above that a platform on which stood Snook, brass pistol still in one hand, the other holding a strap attached to the cables that disappeared into the clouds barely a foot above his head. Despite his slightly concussed state Fitch was beginning to understand how this very apparatus might have been used to snatch the King from his bedroom a week before. Eight foot up in the air on the platform Snook waved his pistol little more than not at all.

'I would stay and chat, but I really must be off now, I have plans for the King you see. He's the rather lovely bait in my really wonderfully contrived trap.' He paused for half a breath. 'To the south are the sheer cliffs of Cloud Island, to your north is the arctic circle. Don't say I didn't offer you any help.' He smirked merely a fraction and without so much as a wave, clicked a relay by his left hand and with barely a whisper the great iron drill began to ascend back up into the clouds.

Realising his backside was getting a bit cold on the ice, Fitch tried to stand. The woman moved quickly and with surprising strength to help him up and he gave a re-assuring thumbs-up in thanks. She responded in kind and then circled her finger to ask what direction they thought they ought to move, since staying still seemed not an option. He shrugged somewhat forlornly realising he could see only white in all directions and the light was probably starting to fade a little. Still any direction was better than none, so he picked one and began to trudge that way with heavy feet, still feeling somewhat dazed. He was just beginning to find some speed and adjust his bootee-clad feet to the icy conditions below when he walked with force and an almighty metallic crash into something solid, iron and as unrelentingly white as the clouds and ice around them.

'Oh what the buggering hell now,' he muttered disconsolately before slipping rapidly, and with some relief, into unconsciousness.

When he came to, Fitch was surprised to find himself lying on a not uncomfortable hospital bed in relatively warm and mercifully stable surroundings.

'Ah, our patient is recovering,' came warm pleasant tones from off to one side, followed by a slightly more disconcerting 'THROW HIM OVERBOARD!' that sounded like a screeching animal of some hideous demeanour. Fitch blinked to clear his vision and take in the smiling face of what was clearly a fit-looking, sea-faring man of some description, complete with neatly trimmed dark beard and heavy naval sweater. Somewhat more puzzling was the bedraggled form of a stuffed and mouldy old parrot that seemed to be perched on the man's shoulder. It was an odd visage indeed. The rest of the room appeared to be a very well appointed, if a little musty, ship's infirmary replete with all the mod cons such a thing might offer.

'Chief Stoker Second Class Marcus Flavius Octavian Hildengraph Smith at your service,' intoned said seaman cheerfully. 'Call me Stanley if you like. Welcome to my boat, take no notice of old Quentin Beakface here.' With this he tipped a wink towards the decrepit inanimate fowl on his shoulder. Then without breaking metaphorical stride, and not really attempting to throw his voice as such he added out of the side of his mouth in the weird screeching bird-voice 'HE'S A BABOON, A SMELLY BABOON I TELL YOU!' Since Fitch found himself rendered somewhat speechless by this, Stanley carried on undaunted. 'Your colleague Lilly here tells me you've been looking for the King of all people,' he stated jovially and then squawked 'PERVERT!' Not really having the strength or desire to get into the whole parrot situation, Fitch decided to focus more on the revelation of the oriental woman's name.

'How do you know her name's Lilly?' he growled.

'I told him, naturally,' explained Lilly in rather pleasing plummy tones. 'I assumed you were some kind of mad yokel, who probably didn't have much grasp of English.' She added as she stepped forward into his line of sight. 'Sorry about all that pointing and so forth; Lilly Fortitude is the name, King's Agent first class.' She offered a strong and well-manicured hand, which Fitch shook somewhat groggily.

'Tobias Fitch, hired gun,' was all he could offer in return.

'Very glad to make your acquaintance at last.' She beamed. 'The Stoker here has brought me up to date, let me catch you up too.' With this she proceeded to explain that the vessel into which Fitch had walked at pace was in fact the enormous New Albion steamship and icebreaker – SS Unstoppable Progress – which had become rather inconveniently, and extremely ironically, stuck fast in the ice whilst exploring the northern passage (or 'The Great White' as it is commonly called) some five or so years before. The captain and most of the crew had set off in a burst of unrestrained optimism to fetch help and never been seen since. Leaving only the preposterously over-nomenclatured Chief Stoker Smith to look after things. Then, when the stoker had popped out to answer a call of nature, she added conspiratorially that whilst the stoker himself seemed right as rain, his parrot-fixated alter-ego seemed to be as demented as a box of the proverbials. She helped Fitch to sit upright on the bed and fetched him an ice-cold glass of water, which he took gratefully.

'Am I right in assuming you, like me, were instructed to look for the King?'

'Spot on old chap.' Expanding to her theme she went on to explain how she had engineered an introduction to Snook and his conspirators whilst posing as a passing diplomat and possible ally. Snook had even shown her around his giant airship craft before a traitor working in the ship's kitchens had blown her cover. 'It really is quite a vessel floating up there, nearly the size of a small town.' Fitch grunted his acknowledgement of this. 'It's not going anywhere in a hurry though y'know.' she had his full attention now.

'Really, how do you know that?'

'Well, I have this,' and from nowhere in particular she produced an ornate brass key and placed it into Fitch's outstretched hand. 'It's the ignition key, no less. During my tour I managed to purloin it.' Fitch didn't enquire how, but he was impressed up to a point.

'Very good, I'm sure, but I imagine they can hotwire it without too much delay.'

'Perhaps,' she smirked, 'but not without their only soldering iron.' And with a flourish she produced a gas-powered heavy duty brass soldering iron and tossed it onto the bed.'

'Okay, also impressive, but I still imagine...' he didn't finish the sentence as she once again produced an even larger brass and copper object and tossed this also on the bed with a heavier thump. 'What in the dickens is that?'

'Oh that, it's just their main relay fuse. Probably bought us at least another hour with that little lot.' Fitch shook his head in both wonder and confusion. He was about to enquire just exactly how she had managed to purloin these items, and more to the point exactly where on, or about, her person she had secreted them when Stoker Stanley and parrot arrived back in the room with a cherry, 'Ah, you're up,' and a rather more grotesque 'BURN THE WITCHES EYES' from the "parrot".

Fitch blinked and shook his head a few times. Quite unbelievably it seemed that despite his concussion, the bat-shit-crazy schizoid seaman and the seemingly implausibly light-fingered king's agent's carrying on, a plan was actually being formed in his befuddled mind. Given Agent Fortitude's work though, it would have to be put in to action sharpish so he hauled himself up onto his still be-tighted legs.

'Stanley, or whatever your name is. Are there any weapons on this hulk of yours?'

'Plenty,' sparked up the seaman, 'what are you after? We have a full complement of rifles, pistols, flares and, of course, the triple harpoon launchers in the bow.'

'Of course,' Fitch rubbed his hands eagerly.

'AND THE CUSTARD,' added the "parrot" 'TELL HIM ABOUT THE CUSTARD!'

'Get them all,' barked Fitch, unfazed by thoughts of killer desserts. Before the Seaman could act on his commands though he further enquired, 'this is a paddle steamer is it not? Do your engines still run stoker?'

'It is and they do sir, although we'll not be going anywhere in a hurry.'

'That won't be necessary, fire them up if you will and prepare for full reverse on my command. Then bring the weapons to the bow as quickly as you like.'

'Aye aye sir,' the seaman saluted briskly and turned to go.

'HIS GRANNY HAS NO LEGS!' shrieked the "parrot" in lieu of a more formal goodbye and he was gone to his tasks.

'I assume this plan has a role for me?' enquired Agent Fortitude stepping forward lithely.

'Indeed, the most vital role of all. Make aft and set fire to anything and everything you can find.' Before she could take this in, Fitch was already ushering her out of the door. 'Speed here is vital and you have the best of all of us methinks. This first deed done make haste and gather up parrot-features and as many weapons as you think worthwhile and we'll meet at the harpoons in the bow. No questions, move!' Knowing better than to argue with a direct command she nodded respectfully and also departed. With a deep breath and wondering exactly what he was getting them all into Fitch looked in vain for a pair of trousers and finding exactly none headed for the deck instead.

Arriving amidships between the colossal wrought iron waterwheels that towered over him with their thick covering of ice and snow Fitch had another inspired thought. He knew a little of ships of this class having worked briefly on SS Unsinkable Modernity, just before it sunk, and most were fitted with a giant periscope on the central mast exactly for the purpose of seeing above low cloud. Heartened by hearing the heavy rumble of the engines grinding into life beneath his feet he located the ornate brass eyepiece and gripped the icy side handles. He felt his spirits race as firstly he realised that looking through the scope the weather had indeed changed and above the cloud was now clear and impeccably blue sky. Swivelling the handle round he first located Snook's astonishingly huge airship, clearly going nowhere in a hurry, with no sign of its engines running. Beyond that vessel the crest of Cloud Island also loomed above the clouds, clearly visible in the late evening sunlight. Moving away from the periscope he headed onwards towards the bows, some way distant yet, to prepare the harpoon guns. Although he could not see the stern of the great iron clad through the low-lying clouds the smell of smoke was reaching his nostrils and he assumed that Fortitude had indeed started fires as instructed.

Reaching the bow a minute or two later he found, and began to make ready, the harpoons, relying on the muscle memory from years in the military to get the massive weapons ready to fire. With a sickening lurch he felt the bow suddenly rise a foot or two as the fires aft began to melt the ice field gripping the mighty steamship causing the stern to drop a little. Time to unleash the mighty iron horses of her doughty engines one last time. His task, a little harder now given the incline of the deck and occasional lurch as she tilted further backwards into the ice, Fitch located the forward speaking tube and flipped open its brass cap.

'Engine room!' he yelled and quickly put his ear to the tube.

'Standing by!' came the distant shout by reply.

108

'Good man!' he exclaimed, 'Engines full reverse, then get your self up here as fast as the devil himself!'

'GO FIDDLE WITH YOUR HOSEPIPE, BUCKET MOUTH!!' came the screeched reply that Fitch took to be a confirmation of sorts. He slapped the lid back and with all the speed he could muster found any ropes or lengths of cable he could, secured them one by one to the third of the harpoons and threw them back in the direction of the stern in the hope it would aid the arrival of the others. By this time the angle was approaching thirty degrees and Fitch found himself back in the clouds. There was an astonishingly loud and stomach churning sound of straining metal from the hull of the monstrous ship as an acrid cloud of engine smoke engulfed him for a moment and the deck lurched further off level. Such was the extreme angle that Fitch was forced to hold on for dear life, whilst still trying to prop himself up into a workable position to fire the harpoons. The angle was nearly forty-five degrees as Fitch wedged himself into the space between the harpoons and the arc of the bow itself, swivelling them to port in the position he knew he would need to fire to hit the airship when they cleared the clouds. The air was so thick with cloud, engine and fire smoke that it was almost pitch black and Fitch eyes stung so much he was almost blinded. His only slight relief was that he could detect the light above the clouds coming ever nearer. Then his heart skipped a beat as the ship lurched once more and this time continued steadily moving, the stern well submersed and the whole craft pivoting around the giant waterwheels to push the bow ever further upwards.

'Fortitude?' He called downwards more in hope than expectation.

'Fitch!' Came back a choked cry, distant but not as far away as he had feared. This time the parrot had nothing to add. Relieved that at least one of them was in earshot he added,

'Hold tight, make fast to any rope hanging from my position. Let go for no one and nothing!' He then tied himself to the last harpoon cable and braced once more as with quite a fair amount of speed the bow of the ship broke through the cloud and into the clear air above. Grunting and trying to breath through the clearing smoke he swivelled the gun waiting for the movement of the bow to bring it in line with the airship, still floating forlornly only a few hundred yards away.

'Here goes nothing!' he muttered and pulled the first harpoon fire lever. A great shower of sparks and an electrical explosion nearly blinded him, but the harpoon did not fire! Eyes forced shut by smoke and sparks he fumbled for the second lever and pulled hard. Another dramatic bang, but this time the harpoon was away, streaking hard for the airship envelope. With no time to admire his shot he pushed the final harpoon a little nearer vertical and bellowed downwards into the pitch black with every ounce of volume he could muster,

'Now soldiers! Hold fast!' and pulled the final harpoon lever. A spark, a crackle – nothing – save the air from the arcing bow whistling past his ears, the massive ship very nearly fully vertical in the water. Then a bang and a sickening lurch as the harpoon fired, arcing high into the air dragging Fitch, ropes, cables and, possibly the others, into the air and out over the airship. As he flew Fitch looked back seeing the great bow of the SS Unstoppable Progress fly past the vertical and begin to descend back into the clouds great plumes of white, grey and thick black smoke billowing in all directions. She was on her very last journey to the bottom of The Great White, he just hoped it had all been worth it. He fancied he could indeed make out figures clinging on to the cables flying behind, but before he could think on it more he reached the apogee of his flight and began to drop back through the icy air. Seconds later he landed with a mighty thump on the welcoming canvas of Snook's giant airship. The great arcing cables started to fall on top of him and half a heartbeat later Fortitude and Smith, laden with armaments, crashed right on top and all around him. Something hard hit his head and for the second time that day he passed out cold.

He came to again a little later and was pleased to see a cool blue sky above him and feel a gentle breeze tickling his skin. He pulled himself upright and realised that he was atop the enormous airship drifting and descending slowly (perhaps due to a puncture in one of its mighty gasbags) towards the relative safety of the now sunlit expanses of Cloud Island. Behind him a great vertical plume of black smoke marked the last known position of the SS Unstoppable Progress. The mighty airship's engines were still motionless; they never did manage to get them going, thought Fitch. Fortitude had stitched them up good and proper. A movement caught his eye off to the right. He strained to see and thought for a moment he must be seeing double as quite a way off, on a strange pedal-powered ornithopter there appeared to be *two* Snooks pedalling frantically for all they were worth. How very odd he thought, two of the rat-faced little blighters, and with this he felt a sudden wave of dizziness and promptly passed out yet again.

Whilst Fitch lay unconscious and the giant airship carried out a kind of slow-motion belly flop onto the plains of Cloud Island, Fortitude and Smith (still somehow having retained his stuffed parrot) released the king with the assistance of a company of New Albion Marines who had arrived from the marooned gunship in their own navy airship. The island itself was thus retaken for the Crown and Caruthers-Simpleton, still in his inadequate robe, clapped in irons. Despite frantic searching on the airship and island, no sign of Snook could be found and it was feared he had escaped to plot another day.

The failure to capture Snook and not much of clue as to his motivation in kidnapping the King, except perhaps as a lure to other forces of the Crown, meant the case was not resolved to everyone's liking. Most especially when the tale was relayed to Admiral Sherman the dog shook her head and growled under her breath in annoyance.

When it came time for them all to leave, Agent Fortitude and Chief Stoker Smith came to collect Fitch from his convalescent bedroll in what passed locally as a kind of hospital.

'How are you feeling old chap?' enquired Fortitude resplendent in a yak fur coat, looking as though she'd just stepped off a cruise ship rather than being embroiled in the adventure that had just passed.

'Sore head,' was all he could find strength to mutter in reply. 'King?'

'Safe, rescued, rather taken with the whole escapade.'

'Smith?'

'Present and correct and mighty happy to be finally back on dry land,' piped up Smith in his unnervingly cheery tones.

'I COULD EAT A PICKLED TEA COSY!' he added in his strange parrot voice.

'Hmmm,' muttered Fitch feeling his headache start to throb again, and then finally enquired, 'Snook?'

'Long gone I'm afraid,' reported Fortitude with a little regret in her voice.

'THERE'S TWO OF THE SILLY BUGGERS. TWO I TELL YOU!' squawked the "parrot" without being asked.

Fitch raised an eyebrow vaguely in the stuffed bird's direction. 'For once, the silly old feathered nutter might actually be right,' he muttered, but no one had a clue what he was on about.

VII

La Grande Course de la Caravane

With giddy excitement Ellen Hall skipped eagerly amongst the many exotic delights of the crowd that bustled vibrantly all around her. Keeping her heavy leather satchel tight by her side and clutching both battered carpet bag and dusty sun-hat alike to prevent them being dislodged, she made her way quickly as, by her chronometer, the Grand Depart was barely five minutes hence. All about her acrobats and dancers swayed, fire-eaters breathed sticky flames and merchants offered all kinds of exotic looking sustenance for the journey the fortunate few were about to make. It was a heady mix of smells, sounds and sights that made up this wonderful pageant for greatest race on Earth: La Grande Course de la Caravane (or to give it its more prosaic English translation – The Big Caravan Race) and the greatest sights of all were the marvellous steam, gas and diesel powered sand-haulers preparing to drag their motley caravans over the baking desert to the distant finish line.

These mighty machines were a mishmash of re-purposed steam locomotives, traction engines and other doughty beasts of burden, some built entirely for this purpose alone. All had mighty rubber-rimmed brass sand wheels or, in a few cases, caterpillar tracks for dealing with the harsh desert landscape. The oldest of these haulers were quite a feast for the eyes, their iron bodies painted garishly bright and bedecked with garlands, streamers and flags fluttering in the steam from their snorting boilers. Some even had the most incredible steam-powered orchestras mounted atop their engines: pipes, horns and percussion all powered by excess gases and driven by punched cards that seemed to feature a quaint line in Gallic and Olde Albion folk tunes that were probably big in the day. Dodging a particularly excitable looking snake charmer Ellen glanced down the lines of the engines as she hurried past, taking in the great "caravans" of miscellaneous carriages that stretched out behind each of them. The sight was truly astonishing and it was very hard to take it all in as anticipation for the start seemed to notch up by the second with a great chorus of cries, songs and blasts of exotic "music" from the steam orchestras.

At the front of each of the caravans was the owner, or keenest salesperson, imploring all who looked vaguely half-interested into paying to join their particular train for the race. Ellen dodged past them all with a shimmy and a muttered apology, as her passage had been booked for months on one of the more venerable of the vehicles. In all her three years of exploring and adventuring gone she had always clung on to the dream of making the final leg of this journey in one of the great racing caravans. The escapade ran the full length of the Nubian Desert, somewhere between two and ten days travel, depending on the velocity of your vessel. Of course some ran the race in an attempt to win, but most went for the thrill, the fiesta and, frankly, just to say you'd done it. It was obvious that the great din was building to a crescendo and Ellen was relieved to finally come across her chosen steed, the name of which translated with an astonishing amount of pompous brio to: *Elevated Holy Transport of the Desert God Arganta The Mighty Saviour of All Peoples And Animals*. It was in fact, although you'd do well to recognise it now, an old steam train that once served the *Eastliest Indies Companye* and now boasted one of the most crazy and intricate steam orchestras of all the haulers. Including, as it had been sold her, a full pipe organ and bell-ringing marionettes.

Identifying herself to the porter at her carriage, one of merely four double-decked waggons amongst the twenty or so pulled by this particular engine, she eagerly hauled herself up the worn iron steps to the top floor and sank with relief into a battered leather seat. A secondary reason for selecting this particular vehicle was for this very upper storey to its passenger cars, which allowed wonderful views of the carnival and the race itself. Below her bustling local bakers called out in many tongues the breads and cakes they had for sale, a last chance to stock up for the journey before they left civilisation behind for a few days. Above circled a great circus of multi-coloured kites, airships and blimps buzzing around the starting line like moths around a particularly vigorous flame. Ellen felt her excitement boil up almost fit to burst as the assault on her senses showed not the least sign of diminishing.

She glanced around the hot, dusty carriage, which had seen better days but nothing quite so thrilling as this, taking in the one or two fellow travellers. A religious woman with a starched headdress wouldn't catch her eye, but a pretty young lady in a slightly tatty white dress and desert boots, clutching a small bag tightly to her chest, did offer her a shy wave. It was curious that she should be travelling alone, thought Ellen, who in truth was only a couple of years older than her. Nevertheless she returned the wave and, as she brought her gaze back to the window, made a silent pledge to keep half an eye on her.

Her musings were interrupted by the most ear-popping sound as the much-vaunted steam-powered orchestra that adorned the top of her locomotive gave off a startling blast of chaotic "music". She had to bite her lip to not give out a squeal of sheer ecstasy as, sensing the start was indeed imminent; the locals began to gather up their wares and other paraphernalia and scurry with unseemly haste to get clear of the mighty engines before they lurched forward. Her own crazy vehicle was not one of the fancied runners and was well to the side of the starting line, but this offered her the most amazing views from her elevated seat of all the mighty engines now preparing for the off with great bellows of dirty steam. A shudder ran down the carriages as the engine cranked and belched into life, sending a cloud of hot acrid smoke down over them, forcing Ellen to shield her eyes with an excitable giggle. Crudely amplified voices from an airship somewhere overhead broke through the din, reeling off what was almost certainly a countdown in some local dialect. Screams and cheers from all around added to the cacophony as the fervour levels reached near fever pitch. Then they all jumped in unison as a mighty cannon went off with a shattering boom that briefly drowned out everything else and with a tremendous judder that rattled everything not firmly screwed down (which on this contraption was most things), they were underway! More blasts of music of various levels of tunefulness and cheers accompanied the start as great clouds of dust were kicked up in all directions, causing one and all to cover their faces with scarves and handkerchiefs. The noisiest, smelliest, dirtiest and, indeed, most-bonkers-est race on the planet had begun!

It was several minutes before the dust cleared enough to be able to take in the spectacle around them more clearly. In that time Ellen had befriended the young lady, whose name was Cleanta, and found out a little bit of her story. Her dark skin and flashing green eyes had quite captivated Ellen as she recounted, in quite marvellous English, her tale of travelling to visit relatives in the east and returning with a medium status family heirloom to pay for her education (on which she seemed very keen) and putative marriage (on which she was less so). Like Ellen the caravan race had been an affordable way of returning home in good time, although the risks were obviously scaring her a little.   The girl ran a slender hand through her dark locks as she talked and Ellen decided that the journey was going to be all the more enjoyable for her company.

As the dust cleared further they both moved excitedly to the windows to take in the great vista of the desert, now covered in clanking metal trains moving with increasing speed towards the far horizon and (somewhere very distant) the finishing line. Streamers, kites and flags flew from every engine and blasts from their improvised steam instruments created a quite glorious racket. Ellen and Cleanta had to poke their heads out of the small windows to see the full extent of the immense vehicles, stretching out now as far as you could see in every direction. They grinned like giddy fools at each other and shared a hug for no reason at all other than to congratulate themselves on their good fortune to be a part of it.

Hard as it was to drag oneself away from taking it all in, after an hour or so hunger got the better of them and sandwiches were taken washed down with lukewarm bottles of lemonade purchased from a young native girl who had somehow managed to smuggle herself aboard.   It was in this slight lull that Ellen began to realise that something was not quite right with the nearest caravan to the port side. Generally speaking the great trains of the desert kept parallel lines and the course was, for the most part, very straight indeed since turning was not easily accomplished.   However the next machine across, a similarly crude contraption to their own, had been inching its way nearer to them. The speeds of the two great vehicles were roughly similar and, since braking was also not a trivial matter, it seemed, to an increasingly concerned Ellen, that a collision was becoming more and more likely. Glancing across she could clearly see the equally alarmed looking faces of the other train's paying punters and, for want of something better to do, she waved meekly.

Ahead of her voices were raised in angry shouts, the horns of the locomotive now sounding in urgent warning rather than carnivalesque joy. But all to no avail, as it soon became apparent that each set of engineers was urging the *other* to change course; and all the while the mighty wheels of the two vehicles were converging at an alarming rate. Dust kicked up into the carriage as Ellen, her Air Cadet training kicking in, called a warning to her fellow passengers, 'Brace yourselves!' The notice came none too soon as with a might crash of wheels, screeching strained metal and a melancholy parp from the steam orchestra, the two vehicles collided side on. All were thrown to the floor Cleanta gripping her small leather bag all the tighter to her chest as an almighty judder knocked the wind from her lungs. Despite the collision the vehicles were still moving relentlessly. The *Holy Transporter* however was now heading well off course, having veered nearly ninety degrees to the north dragging the great column of carriages and tenders, at a seasick angle, through the turn behind it. Each one sparking and grating against the other train as they peeled apart.

'What's happening?' asked Cleanta in a remarkably calm voice. To find out Ellen pushed her head back out of the window and looked forward towards the locomotive, hat discarded and goggles now clamped over her eyes, her short blonde hair smeared with dirt.

'Looks like we are still running, but the steering may be broken,' relayed Ellen taking in the increasingly frantic arm waving of the footplate engineers, 'I guess we're going this way for a bit.' Not the best thing for those hoping to reach the western coast at any point in the next few days, but Ellen had read about such things happening in the race and the vehicles were well equipped to cope with any eventualities being pretty much self-sufficient for the duration. Despite now leaning to the right a small amount the carriage was not jerking about so much that checks could not be carried out amongst the passengers to see if much was broken. The half a dozen or so of them in the small upper carriage seemed well enough and cups of tea were ordered via a speaking tube and this relieved the tension somewhat. Ellen used this time to check her own belongings were safe and, just in case, moved her small brass revolver from her satchel and tucked it into her leather belt. She had found on her travels that it was always best to be prepared for the worst.

After she was sure everyone was safe and sound Ellen, accompanied by Cleanta who volunteered very eagerly to join her, made their way down to the nearly deserted lower part of the carriage, then through tenders and tankers with a mission to find someone with knowledge of the situation to identify if there was a plan to get them back on course. At the back of a rattling coal-tender they encountered a dust-smeared native stoker with her dark skin, goggles and protective suit now pitch black with coal dust and grease. After one or two attempts they found a language that both the stoker and Cleanta could converse in and the stoker told them in no uncertain terms that they should not worry in the slightest as the redoubtable and wise captain was an old and learned hand at this and had many, many ways up her rather splendidly tailored sleeve get them back on course in no time at all. In any case, she went on, the desert was immense in its vastness and the likelihood of hitting something bigger than them was beyond remote, but if they did the chances of a savage, grinding death were nothing that they should concern themselves with it in the slightest. Oh and while she thought of it, desert wolves were not particularly likely to find their injured bodies and rip them limb from limb, no, no that was unlikely in the extreme and they should not bother themselves with that either, not even a smidgeon. Not particularly mollified by any of this, but discouraged from going any further to get a more prosaic synopsis, they reluctantly began to make their way back on the shaking gangways.

Between a workshop tender, now bustling with mechanics that seemed to be arguing loudly and with much animation about what action was required to fix the ailing machine, and a large water tanker, was a ladder that led up onto the carriage roof. Cleanta flashed her green eyes through her dark lashes at Ellen and gave a quick glance up and down the corridor for officials.

'I fancy we'll get a better view from up there,' she whispered mischievously. Ellen had, in truth, been thinking the same thing and needed no further convincing.

'Too right, let's go quickly before someone comes,' and so they clambered up, Cleanta first and Ellen, after a further sly glance around, quickly after her. As she poked her head up above the roof she was surprised to find that there were three young urchins sitting up there checking their takings and stock in small hampers that they had been dragging around the train. They were alarmed at first and looked ready to leg it along the roof, but Ellen smiled and offered a cheery handshake and they soon realised they not going to be evicted and so proceeded to ignore them completely. The view from the top of the carriage was indeed a sight to behold. The great desert vistas stretched out as far as the eye could see to all points of the compass. In front of them the *Holy Whatnot,* with its steam funnel and the wacky instruments of its orchestra, dominated the view. Behind stretched out the rag-tag assembly of the caravan and beyond their cloud of dust they could just about make out the great plumes of steam and glinting kites from the great race itself now streaming at a ninety degree angle to them and getting more distant by the minute. Putting aside her mild alarm at this aspect, Ellen found herself otherwise quite captivated by the whole panorama and she was only brought back to earth by Cleanta tugging urgently on the sleeve of her shirt.

'Erm, any idea what those might be?' she asked with only a hint of concern, pointing her lean arm towards several plumes of dust pretty much dead ahead. Accompanying these was an ominous dark shape in the air, that was, more than likely, an airship of some kind although it was still hard to tell through the steam from the great coal-fired engine ahead.

'Nothing good I'll wager,' offered Ellen first checking her pistol was still safe and then pulling an extending brass travel-o-scope from her satchel. Squinting through this she tried to make out the shapes through the dust clouds and heat haze ahead. The dark blob was indeed an airship and through the telescope she could make out it had a fish-like shape with great canvas fins and a mean-looking shark's teeth and eyes painted on the front. The great metal cabin below was an armoured military type and seemed to be bristling with rockets, harpoons and cannon pointing in all directions. Ellen tried to swallow, but her throat was dry and the dust only made it sting, her heart was thumping rapidly now beneath her grimy shirt. Looking lower she could now begin to make out the shapes on the desert floor kicking up great plumes of gritty sand behind them.

'War horses!' she exclaimed not realising she was speaking aloud. Right enough they were indeed great steam-powered iron war-horses. She knew them well enough from her time in the cadets, they had once been state-of-the-art military hardware, but they had long been superseded by superior technology. Shifting her gaze back she realised that the airship was a similar vintage to the horses. An armoured air-monitor that was cutting edge maybe half a century before. She could begin to make out people in the cabin and on "horse" back – dark-skinned natives, with war paint smeared crudely on their faces.

'Pirates!' she exhaled and lowering the telescope she realised that the urchins were long gone and she and the dusky girl were the only ones left on the roof. 'We should warn the others,' but before she could do anything, a mighty flash of light and flame came from the wicked looking airship followed by a booming bark of thunder. Seconds later a rocket hit the *Holy Which-a-me-call-it* and, in a blinding flash of light and sparks, the front wheels were blown off and the whole edifice buried its head into the unforgiving sand. This in turn caused a stomach-churning judder to run down the spine of the caravan as carriages and tenders alike shunted into each other like toppling dominos, throwing Ellen and Cleanta off the roof and down with a thump onto the desert floor. Dazed and confused they barely had enough time to dust themselves off before the first of the great iron horses loomed threateningly over them. Standing nearly fifteen feet tall the mighty machine was composed of a steam engine with a round black boiler for a belly. A funnel, coughing out acrid clouds of black smoke, rose like an iron tail from the rear, and the crude animal shaped head with an ornate cannon protruding from the snout arched down towards them. The mechanoid had four rusty articulated metal legs at the front and another set in mirror configuration at the rear. In some ways more like a giant armoured crab than the cobs that gave the machine its name. Atop this mechanical marvel were four or five Berbers in a mixture of local desert clothes and, somewhat oddly, remains of Olde Albion military uniforms. Their faces were painted with stripes and angled lines, which matched the menacing decorations of their horse and airship that now drifted overhead blocking the sunlight. Ellen grabbed frantically for her pistol, but found to her horror that she had lost it in the fall. She still had her satchel though and moved with alacrity to bury it behind the nearest half-covered giant wheel before the pirates could get to her. With whoops and bloodthirsty cries they had leapt from the iron machines and moved quickly with glistening cutlasses and mean-looking flintlocks to the passenger sections, looking to relieve the travellers of anything of value. Fortunately despite their array of ancient, but still very deadly, weaponry and paramilitary demeanour no one was harmed and no hostages were taken. Indeed the only dicey moment came when a particularly savage looking pirate lunged to take Cleanta's small leather pouch. Her eyes had widened and she had tightened her muscles into a fighting stance before Ellen moved to restrain her, as a vibrating sabre was shaken with great menace in her general direction.

'You can't win this one brave girl,' whispered Ellen holding her head close to Cleanta's dark locks, 'let's live to fight another day.' With extreme reluctance Cleanta released her white-knuckled grip and her bag was taken to join the other booty. Then, having scared everyone half to death and rallied by the blood-curdling cry of the Pirate Queen, the pirates remounted their iron steads and began to retreat. As the mechanoids began to lumber away from them and the airship leaned lazily overhead beginning its u-turn, Ellen was shocked to see Cleanta gather up her bustling skirts and begin to stride after them with great purpose.

'Where are you going?' she hissed as she scurried to retrieve her precious satchel, dusting the sand off it, and then scampered after her.

'I *cannot* lose what's in that bag,' she muttered darkly over her shoulder not even turning to face the panting adventurer as she finally caught her up.

'What's so important about a family heirloom that you would risk your life?' she asked struggling to keep up in the soft sand.

'There's more to it than that, I've sworn to bring the contents of that bag home at all costs. Do not try to stop me!' she had barely broken stride in this time but the iron horses were rapidly pulling away, and the slower lumbering airship had completed its turn and was once again blocking the harsh desert sun as it throbbed ominously overhead. So determined was she that Ellen thought better of trying to dissuade her, instead her thoughts turned to more cunning ideas.

'We'll die out here on foot, I have a better idea,' and with that she pulled from her satchel a somewhat battered but still rather nifty-looking handgun with a brass harpoon loaded in the barrel and a short length of rope attached, which she proceeded to aim at a section of crudely repaired wooden planking towards the back of the airship gondola. 'Here goes nothing!' she muttered and with that she aimed and fired.

After a somewhat ticklish ascent on Ellen's Handheld Harpoon and Clockwork Climbing Contraption to the belly of the great airship, Ellen and Cleanta had discovered that the wooden panel was actually part of an unused bomb-bay. They had prised it open just enough for the pair of them to crawl inside and were able to relax a little for the remainder of the bumpy journey. By turns the airship arrived at the pirate's lair and was tethered, with a reasonable amount of proficiency, low enough for the pirates to descend on rickety rope ladders. Dusk was sending its shadows over the rocky terrain now and a brief sandstorm sent the rascals scurrying into shelter. Peering tentatively down through a narrow gap in the planks Ellen waited until the coast was clear, then they eased the panel aside so she could stick her head out to look around.

'We seem to be in some sort of giant crater,' reported Ellen. 'Though it's hard to make it all out in this light. There are lamps lit in rooms over to the side,' she continued in subdued tones, 'and the war horses are all corralled near the entrance.'

'Any guards or sentries posted?' enquired Cleanta sounding very business-like.

'None that I can see, either they fear more storms or they feel safe enough here to not deem them necessary.' She pulled her head back into the gloomy bay to find, to her mild surprise, that Cleanta was tugging off her skirts. Underneath she had a very smart looking pair of khaki shorts and strapped to her slim, wiry leg was a small holster with a tiny chrome pistol that was so shiny it glinted even in the half-light.

'If the coast is still clear, perhaps you would be kind enough to help me descend on your harpoon rope,' she enquired, seemingly now ready for a serious undertaking.

'Naturally, but don't think for one minute I'm letting you go about this alone.' Cleanta seemed reluctant to allow this at first, but in the end shrugged in what Ellen took to be a moderately positive manner. 'It's agreed then.' With no contradiction coming Ellen dropped the rope through the bomb-bay doors and they made ready to descend.

After reaching the ground they moved with all speed to the shelter of the nearest wall of the crater and began to take in their surroundings before working out what on earth they might do next. Sure enough they were in a great walled circle, which had an appearance somewhere between an extinct volcano and a medieval fort. The structure was fully three hundred yards across and had probably once been some sort of settlement or perhaps a scientific facility. The walls themselves now had the natural appearance of rock, but could possibly have been human-made originally and just extremely weathered. Here and there some towers and perhaps gantries or other structures were part submerged in the sand, but their function was obscure and none of it made any sense to either of them.

'What do you think this place was?' asked Ellen her goggles now around her neck as the gloom continued to descend.

'Hard to say, but I'd put money on it being some sort of military camp,' hissed Cleanta under her breath.

'I think you are right, those war mechs and the pirate's uniforms are straight out of the history books,' indeed Ellen had even trained on similar models, as the cadets never got the latest kit. Moving carefully so as to not make a sound they edged up to the window of the lamp-lit room and cautiously peered in. Inside the pirates, women, men and even a few children were making merry, laughing and drinking no doubt revelling in a successful raid on the caravan. They appeared entirely oblivious to the two young stowaways and seemed to be totally off their guard; clearly they were not worried about anything interrupting their merriment.

'I see my bag!' hissed Cleanta as quietly as she could given this exciting discovery. 'But it looks discarded, empty. The contents must be stowed elsewhere.'

'We need to get in and take a look,' suggested Ellen leaning in close to her so they could conspire quietly.

'I'm thinking we need some sort of diversion, any ideas?' Ellen was rarely short of an idea or two, and glancing around at the iron horses and airship a cunning albatross of a plan started to unfurl its wings before her.

'I imagine that the loss of their airship and mechanoids will get their attention, don't you think?' she winked at Cleanta feeling adrenaline surge through her body.

'Without doubt,' grinned Cleanta back, 'what do we do?' In hushed tones Ellen outlined the plan at length and, when she was confident that Cleanta understood her part and they had checked the pirates were still unaware of their presence, they moved to make it so. Splitting up and keeping low, Ellen crept towards the six iron horses whilst Cleanta hustled with speed towards the airship. Working with the discipline and wits that had always been her way Ellen moved first to the horse on the far right and taking a spare harpoon from her satchel she jammed it into a joint in right hand front leg. Then she quickly gathered up any rocks or heavy material she could find and crammed the panniers on the same side as full as she could. By the time this had been completed Cleanta came up, glistening with sweat, hauling the tether rope still attached to the airship behind her. With silent signals and the odd whisper they tied the airship to the left-a-most horse and then Ellen set about showing her sister-in-arms how to prime the steam engines. She was pleased to find that, despite their generally laconic air, the pirates had left the fireboxes alight and very little needed to be done to get them going. When all was prepared as best as they could they met again by the middle horses.

'Right, three horses each, start them and send them going. Then raise the alarm in the dialect you used on the train and dive for the shadows when all hell breaks out!' The nerves were really kicking in now and Ellen began to shake a little as they started each horse in turn and sent them clanking off out into the desert wastes. Ellen expected to see the pirates come charging out at the first sound, but it soon became apparent that even Cleanta screaming blue murder from the side of the cavern brought nary a single soul out to see what was occurring. By this time the horses were beginning to gather speed and, towing the airship along with them, trotting out into the gloom. Despairing slightly that their diversion was not really yielding the desired effect the two tried yelling again at the top of their voices, but still nothing. Finally in frantic desperation Cleanta took up a rock and hurled it through the nearest window before ducking urgently back into the shadows.

This finally had the required outcome and, somewhat drunk and in total disarray, the pirates came stumbling out to see what all the commotion was. In utter and complete confusion they spotted their disappearing machines and charged after them waving half empty bottles and cutlasses alike and screaming base profanities in all directions. Without a further word or glance between them Ellen and Cleanta peered carefully into the now deserted mess hall and then ducked inside. As Ellen kept a careful watch, Cleanta searched with surprising discipline and efficiency but found absolutely, precisely: bugger all.

'It's not here, we need to look in the other rooms,' she hissed as Ellen nodded her agreement.

'Split up or together?' she enquired with urgency.

'Together I think – lead on,' and with that Ellen moved to the only other doorway, hauled it open and gave a sudden yelp of surprise. Behind the door, looking only slightly bemused by the whole situation was a dark-skinned girl of about ten, who seemed quite taken by the exotically pale blonde woman confronting her. Selecting diplomacy over brute force Ellen blurted, 'Oh hello there!'

'Hello,' replied the child rather nonplussed.

'I'm Ellen, who are you?'

'Simone, I'm nine,' replied the girl in perfect English starring at Ellen with wide brown eyes.

'Oh right, that's very good,' responded Ellen, holding out an arm to reassure Cleanta who had started to advance, pistol in hand, behind her. 'And this is Cleanta, we're looking for something of hers, that's all really and then we'll toddle off.' The child considered this for a second or two, tipping her head to one side to help her thought processes, such as they were. Then after a while she chirped,

'Well it's probably in *The Sink*,' and with not a syllable more she turned on her heels and skipped off down the corridor. Shrugging to each other the two adventurers followed cautiously but quickly lest the girl think better of helping them, and by turns they came to a room with a heavy barred door that looked much like a vault. Fortunately the door was not locked and they all went inside to find "The Sink" which was in fact a large hole in the floor filled with glinting treasure. However their luck ran out, as the grille and the ladder for accessing it were both securely locked. The only other thing in the room was a large copper-ringed water tank with heavy lead pipes leading off into the wall.

'Don't suppose you have a key for this?' enquired Cleanta thinking it worth the question at least. At the same time she peered down into the pit, where a miscellaneous array of items appeared to have been thrown both willy and indeed nilly. The girl shook her head and shrugged and this was taken to be a negative response in relation to the key enquiry. Despite this Cleanta pointed excitedly into the pit, 'I see it!' she exclaimed, 'it's there, we just need a way to get it out.'

'When I grow up I'm going to be an sailor,' ventured the girl randomly.

'Oh right,' offered Ellen looking only slightly flummoxed at this potential career choice, but somehow it triggered a thought in her. 'Cleanta – would you wager your heirloom is heavier or lighter than water?' she called out to her lithe friend who was trying in vain to reach down through the grille.

'Eh? Er, lighter I guess. It's kind of like a valve.'

'Result!' exclaimed Ellen, and putting aside nagging thoughts as to why a family heirloom might be "kind of like a valve" she winked at the still slightly dopey looking girl, 'give us a hand then squirt'. And with that she proceeded, with the child's help, to usher Cleanta out of the way and womanhandle the overflow pipe from the water tank into the hole. Turning the tap she then started to pour water in, Cleanta gave her a big smile.

'Ah, now there's a good idea, we'll float it out'

'Exactly,' confirmed Ellen, although the hole must have been very deep as it was taking quite a long while to fill up with water, and it could only be a matter of time before they might be discovered by someone more anxious to stop them than their laconic child companion. To pass the anxious moments she decided to quiz the girl who was still seemingly not in the least bit bothered by all the evening's goings on.

'So tell me Simone, what is this place exactly?'

'Well I'm not really supposed to say,' muttered the girl somewhat diffidently but decided to say anyway, 'Mummy says it's top secret. Apparently some people used to pay us to guard it, you know scare people off and stuff.'

'I see,' mused Ellen rubbing her ample chin, 'don't suppose you know who those "some people" might be?' The girl shrugged again, seemingly her favourite gesture. 'Thought not, but presumably they supplied all these uniforms, weapons and machines?' The girl nodded her affirmation of the hypothesis. 'Then we have a pretty big clue I think.' Cleanta was still stretching to reach her object but she nodded that she was thinking the very same thing. 'You say these people *used* to pay you, so what happened?' The girl shrugged one more time, but this time there were accompanying words:

'Mummy said the money just stopped coming. This was ages ago, way before I was born. Since then mummy just takes stuff off people.'

'Like the great caravan race!' chipped in Cleanta.

'The what?' asked the girl looking somewhat on the confused side of totally ignorant.

'Never you mind. I've got it!' and with that Cleanta stood up and held the dripping object, which did indeed resemble a small diode valve and looked exactly nothing at all like a piece of jewellery or similar heirloom. 'What's the plan now?' she asked but there was not a nanosecond for Ellen to respond to this before, with a large crash and a yell, a giant figure burst into the room.

'What is the meaning of all this?' yelled the Pirate Queen, resplendent in a mixture of native costume, Albion General's tunic and customised body armour. A great feathered headdress on her head and, now slightly smeared, war paint still adorning her face. Her eyes bulged with fierce anger, and possibly excessive alcohol, and in her hand was a vicious looking sabre.

'Abandon plan!' was all Ellen could offer, but Cleanta moved with great speed to grab the child and put her pistol to her head.

'Stand back, or I'll not be responsible for my actions,'

'WHAT!' shrieked the Pirate Queen ferociously, but it soon became apparent she would not attack them whilst they had the, still not particularly bothered, child as hostage.

'Sorry about all this,' whispered Ellen to Simone, but true to form the girl simply shrugged. Still blazing fury from every pore the Pirate Queen was forced to move to one side as first Ellen and then Cleanta with the girl in tow squeezed past her, apologetically, and out into the corridor. Safely extracted they quickly bolted the hefty door and released the girl who still seemed to be taking it all in her stride.

Ellen reached into her pocket for a shilling and tossed it to her, as there came a great hammering on the oak door behind them.

'Give us about ten minutes if you would be so kind, then let her out.'

'Sure,' shrugged the girl compliantly, but our heroines were already well down the corridor.

'Oh and good luck with the whole sailor thing,' added Ellen encouragingly, but by now they were out of the door and into the mess hall, so if there was anything other than continued indifference in reply they did not hear it.

'Curious girl,' muttered Cleanta as they made their way out into the dark and towards the gap in the crater where the horses had been tethered. There was no immediate sign of the other pirates and it seemed likely they were still aimlessly pursuing their vehicles somewhere out in the night. 'So far so good, what now?'

'Well...' said Ellen straining her eyes to see through the dark, 'I might have something up my sleeve'. She began to head to the right, still squinting to see into the darkness.

'Erm, what might that be then?'

'Ah, you'll see,' she said semi-confidently and then added 'hopefully' under her breath. With this she started to run further out across the scree in the vague direction of a curious rumbling sound. Cleanta followed her closely, not wanting to lose her in the dark before this mysterious plan had been unveiled.

'What am I supposed to be...' Cleanta's voice tailed off as charging towards them through the gloom came a great lumbering metal machine kicking sand in all directions.

'Run!' yelled Ellen urgently, flashing back past her and Cleanta quickly turned tail and galloped at full speed in pursuit. Before she could shout further enquires though the iron war horse was practically on top of them, Ellen matched its speed as near as she could and grabbed desperately at the harness as the horse continued to clump onwards in a wide circle. The leather straps slipped tantalisingly through her fingers and she bashed her arm against the metal boiler making it go numb. Before she could yell or feel anything in the way of pain, with astonishing speed the lithe body of Cleanta was around her, grabbing the straps and hauling them up onto the first step of the loading ladder. This smart and speedy move confirmed what Ellen felt she already knew: that this girl was no travelling waif, but clearly a highly trained operative of some sort. Working together almost as one body they scrambled up the boiler and onto the seating area on top. Ellen kicked the harpoon out of the disabled front leg and quickly jettisoned the panniers. With this the horse corrected its lopsided course and began to run straight again.

Ahead of them they suddenly saw the furious and clearly extremely agitated form of the Pirate Queen! A gleaming vibro-cutlass in one hand and a great brass blunderbuss in the other, blocking their way and screaming hideous oaths into the desert air.

'That was never ten minutes!' moaned Ellen, but despite frantic attempts to change course they were still heading straight for their nemesis, who levelled the flintlock and fired a screaming volley of buckshot towards them. The iron warhorse could cope with such trifles and the shot bounced and ricocheted off in all directions. Unluckily a piece of shrapnel caught Ellen's still numb arm and she nearly lost her seating as blood began to stain her sleeve. Cleanta grabbed her other arm and tugged her back upright as the iron horse galloped just past the Pirate Queen, who first hurled the empty blunderbuss at them and then reached out and grabbed Cleanta's leg! With blood-curdling screams and yells from all and with Ellen and Cleanta holding on for dear life, they did their best to kick Cleanta's leg free. Just as they thought they would all be pulled down on to the sand, the Pirate Queen lost her grip and fell with a heavy thud onto the ground. All the while the horse continued its relentless galloping and it seemed with one final ear-bursting yell ringing out into the pitch-black night that she had finally given up the pursuit.

'Seriously though,' mumbled Ellen, now half in shock, 'that really was never ten minutes!'

Gathering their composure and locating the compass on the mechanoid's brass dashboard, Ellen grabbed the steering levers and hauled them to make the horse change course and take them away from the pirate base. For a while she ran at an angle to their preferred direction, just until they were definitely out of visual and audible range. Then she slowed the engine to a lower level to save fuel and corrected their course back towards where she estimated that the stricken caravan would still be beached.

When they felt confident they had made good their escape, and had recovered their breath, our two adventurers shared a long hug and then Cleanta patched up Ellen's wounded arm as best she could.

'That was quite some work making the horse run in a great circle to come back to us!' complemented Cleanta scarcely able to believe it had actually worked. 'We'll make a King's agent of you yet.'

'Which is, of course, what you are,' muttered Ellen feeling very drained.

'Got me there,' replied Cleanta bobbing slightly with the motion of the giant ironclad. 'And I'm sure you've guessed that what I was carrying is no family heirloom.'

'Indeed, do you know what it is exactly?' enquired Ellen feeling drowsy but vindicated.

'Not a clue, but if I had to guess given its size and construction, it's not a human artefact.' Ellen felt a shiver go down her spine, the Martian War was ancient history now and most people had blocked the thought of it from their minds, it was a rude awakening to be reminded of that awful time. She shook her head to try and throw the dark thoughts off, but another nagging idea was worming its way into her brain.

'Do you think that pirate outpost has something to do with the War too?'

'I wouldn't bet against it,' offered Cleanta, 'it looked old enough to be something that was abandoned around that time; I guess we'll never know though - if it was, it will be highly classified.' Ellen nodded, knowing this to be true, but couldn't help speculating to herself what an Olde Albion installation was doing all that way out in the desert. Troubled by these thoughts, but comforted by Cleanta's strong wiry arms around her she eventually drifted off into an uneasy slumber. Fortunately she had done her work well so they would eventually see the lights of their caravan glinting in the distance.

It was after nearly two hours of travelling that they arrived at the wrecked sand hauler and the battered caravan of the somewhat less *Elevated Holy Transport of the Desert God Arganta The Mighty Saviour of All Peoples And Animals.* The crew were either too busy arguing with each other, or fast asleep, to even notice their approach. Gathering up the last of her energy Ellen slowed the mighty iron horse and brought it to a halt near the still well and truly mangled steam engine. A further plan had formed during their journey and with Cleanta's rough translation and some, seemingly obligatory, mad arm waving, they convinced the captain that, despite its venerable age, the war horse had more than enough torque to haul the passenger carriages onwards whilst leaving the engineers and their workshop waggons to their repairs. In addition to this they also managed to convince her that the pirates were probably either still frantically chasing their vehicles through the desert, or sleeping off a hangover somewhere, and were very unlikely to be bothering them any time soon.

And so it was that as dawn broke, following careful instruction from Ellen, Cleanta and one of the less demonstrative engineers piloted the warhorse, with half the carriages tethered behind, onwards towards the far westerly Nubian coast. Ellen herself was propped up in the least damaged passenger car drifting slowly in and out of sleep with the bumpy motion. Her arm freshly bandaged from the wonderfully well-stocked medical car, Ellen's fatigued mind was now swirling with thoughts of Martians, abandoned forts in the desert and beautiful dusky girls that turned out to be secret agents. And although she couldn't help feeling some dread at what it all meant, at least, she consoled herself, she could now tell everyone that she had, in somewhat unorthodox fashion, completed the greatest race on earth.

VIII

In The Shadow Of The Moon – Part 2

Still very much dazed and even more confused, Tobias Fitch tried to force his gummed up eyes open just a little to take in his surroundings. He had no idea how long he had been unconscious and, as yet, no memories were demisting themselves enough to allow him to recall how he got to that particular state in the first place. Trying to ignore the throbbing that seemed to come from almost every part of his body he dragged one of his eyelids open and waited groggily as everything gradually came into focus. The first thing that he realised was that he was in the open air and lying on some sort of, extremely uncomfortable, metal table or trolley. Above him he could make out a crescent shape drifting lazily amongst the clouds. Ah, the moon, he thought, it was at least a familiar thing to focus on whilst he allowed his other senses to come back on-line. He became aware of noises around him: hammering and grinding and the general discordant melody of construction. Not too loud or insistent, just enough to let him know that something was being built nearby. He tried to move his arms, but was dismayed to find that they were strapped to the cold metal construction beneath him, however his legs gave every impression of being unrestrained despite the fact he could not move them very much. He had no further time to consider his predicament before he heard footsteps moving fairly swiftly towards him and the sound of something fairly chunky being dragged along behind. Despite throbbing pain from pretty much every part of his neck and shoulders he craned his head towards the sounds and his other eye popped open in surprise at the sight of begoggled man, with wispy grey hair, looming over him, busying himself with lighting a rather gothic looking oxy-acetylene torch.

'Hey waidaminuty thur!' gurgled Fitch desperately trying to wriggle his arms free to defend himself.

'Oh do restrain yourself,' came back a drawling monotone voice that was so dull it almost sent him back into unconsciousness. 'I will not injure you if you hold still.' Despite its overwhelming tediousness the voice had the ring of truth and Fitch decided to do as he was bid and save his strength for now, in any case he realised that the straps holding his arms extended right over his chest and he was going nowhere in a hurry. With surprising deftness the balding man with a rat like nose quickly wielded the torch flame against a chain that appeared to be attached to his hand and a weight, which Fitch had only just become aware of, was removed from his wrist. His eyes were clearing all the time and Fitch could now see that the man had cut the bindings that had fastened an attaché case to his wrist and, having placed the same on a handy workbench, was now proceeding to force it open. The flame of the torch flickered against his vole-like features and Fitch realised that he recognised the face from somewhere.

'I flnow oo,' garbled Fitch racking his dim, but slowly reviving, brain for some sort of clue.

'Give great care on opening case,' came a bizarrely accented voice and another figure stepped into Fitch's field of vision. This one he recognised with a start that sent jangling memories of trains, taxis and ornithopters rampaging back into his sore head. The man had dark features with tight curls on his head and, most tellingly, an ornate moustache that Fitch remembered all too well.

'How, what, when?' spluttered Fitch in his general direction and then reprised superfluously, 'How?' The moustachioed man, resplendent in a velvet smoking jacket ignored his snivelling entirely and instead bent over to inspect the contents of the now open attaché case. The mouse-featured man, who seemed to be dressed entirely in grey from his drab lab coat to his uninspiring shoes, removed his goggles and reached into the case to pull out what seemed to be a small diode valve (or similar) and held it up in two bony fingers to allow the other man to look more closely.

'Attend with maximum care,' intoned the second man with, both comically and eerily, an entirely different accent to when he had spoken previously.

'Naturally I do not wish to damage the very last piece of our Ascension Engine,' drawled the grey figure in his usual drab tones. 'You may desist with your admonishments.'

Meantime the very mention of the word "ascension" had sent a shiver down Fitch's spine and he finally managed to place the grey-coated man, who was surely none other than Wrenish Snook a member of the much-feared Fourth Day Ascension League. It seemed that the case he had been carrying obviously contained something of very great value to them, but chillingly the talk of a machine being near completion troubled him the most.

'Snook!' growled Fitch, feeling his spirits lift a little as adrenaline pumped through his veins. With a throaty yell he threw himself against his restraints to see if he could break free, but with no success. Nevertheless Snook did give a little yelp and step backwards, nearly dropping the glistening glass capsule. The moustachioed man, without showing any obvious signs of alarm, stepped in with a dancer's elegance and took it from him.

'Surfeit of care applied, permit Ian to intercede,' drawled moustache man in yet another different, and completely unplaceable, accent. Didn't really have him down as an Ian, thought Fitch, but he kept this irrelevant insight to himself. Despite his groggy state his instincts were beginning to re-assert themselves, and it was clear he needed to find out as much information as he could about where he was and what was going on. A cunning ploy or sneaky deception was required, so he rummaged deep within the recesses of his, still throbbing, grey matter and found: not-a-dickie-squiggle. So he went for plan B instead,

'Where am I and what is going on?' he asked as civilly as he could muster, as his mother had told him once that politeness always pays and, surprisingly, it seemed to do the trick.

'Well since you ask so nicely,' responded Snook, whilst cautiously double-checking that Fitch's restraints were still very much secure. 'And you are possibly not long for this world, allow me to fill you in.' Before Fitch could quiz him further on this implied threat to his body corporeal, Snook pulled a large metal lever that swung the whole apparatus to which Fitch was attached into an upright position, so that he could see the incredible contraption laid out before them.

They were in the garden of a reasonably well-appointed city house and configured in a circle some thirty feet or so across was a rather mind-boggling array of instruments, pipes and multi-coloured braided wiring laid out across a fretwork iron frame. Copper and brass tubes, clearly supplying electricity and perhaps fluids of some sort snaked across the shrubberies towards the buildings. Laid out in the centre of the circle was an elaborate flooring of some exotic-looking material that glistened like a pearl as the light of the early afternoon sun caught it. Working away on parts of this bizarre edifice were two more men who looked remarkably like Ian the Moustache, in fact they looked so identical that Fitch's brain was struggling to comprehend it all.

'Behold the magnificent Fourth Day Ascension Engine,' intoned Snook joylessly, without any particular sense of occasion. 'A perfect contraption for the invoking of chaos and all the fun that that entails.'

'Sounds like a right barrel of laughs,' muttered Fitch, his eyes flicking this way and that to try and take in the whole landscape and any potential escape routes it might offer. None appeared to present itself, so Fitch decided to carry on with the conversation even though Snook's drab voice was so dull that he might soon become quite keen on passing on to the land immortal. 'How does it work then?'

'Revealing nothing is salient advice,' interjected Ian moustache-features in his odd shifting tones and all three of the triplets turned to stare directly at Fitch with three pairs of eerily unblinking dark brown eyes.

'Alright keep yer wigs on,' muttered Fitch trying not to show how unnerved he was by this whole escapade.

'No idea,' drawled Snook rubbing his thin fingers together in a way that could quite possibly be thought to denote pleasure. 'My understanding is that it either raises the dead, summons ghouls from the other side or tunnels into the core of the earth – Ian has been a little vague about its exact function and utterly silent on the method of its operation. Personally, I care not.' Somewhat mollified by this Ian and his identical colleagues went back to their work. 'We're going to give all three a shot and see what happens.'

'And I guess I'm your sacrificial Chihuahua?' enquired Fitch through gritted teeth.

'Indeed and as the ultimate expression of pure science it will be our great honour to watch and observe the results of this: the final experiment.' He turned towards Ian of the impressive nasal rug who was waiting patiently by a gold and copper box with a receptacle on top that looked a perfect fit for the valve unit from Fitch's case. Snook was warming to his fiendish theme and continued to drawl on as he moved to join him. 'Ian has already worked great wonders with his team, clearing the Metropolis of inhabitants and collating all the items required to build this contraption. We are, naturally, most grateful to you for supplying the last piece of the puzzle, albeit unwittingly.' By this point in the speech Snook's utterly boring jabbering was really starting to get right on Fitch's wick, so much so that he thought his head was going to explode.

'Oh do get on with it then you little weasel!' he blurted, feeling that he'd really rather had it with trying to be civil. Sorry mother.

'Well there is no need to be like that, you did ask.'

'Well I'm unasking, what are you waiting for exactly?'

'Only for my brother to join us, and lo here he is.' Fitch twisted his neck to look in the direction of Snook's gaze and saw another, identical, grey rodent faced man striding with a fair amount of alacrity across an herbaceous border towards the machine.

'Fear not brother dear, I am in attendance. Let the marvels of science begin,' droned the new arrival as he skirted a neatly clipped bay tree and took his place alongside his twin brother.

'Oh for all that is holy, there's two of 'im and three of them!' Fitch was quite done with it all now.

'Indeed, may I introduce my twin brother Rawlish Snook,' droned Wrenish Snook with quite ear-grating dullness.

'I really wish you wouldn't!' muttered Fitch, who had pretty much lost the will to live. 'Just kill me already.' This rather put the kibosh on the ceremonials, so without aught ado of any type the two dull scientists wheeled the trolley arrangement, with Fitch strapped upright on it, into the circle and moved to one of the complicated looking control boxes. Ian and his two identically hirsute companions moved with a kind of robotic elegance to complete the construction and vacate the circular area, taking up positions by the controls without a further word. By the biggest of the panels was an extremely ornate looking brass telescope.

'Ensure positioning of moon in relation to MOO-EAR and confirm same Cynthia,' instructed Ian in his oddly meandering voice and one of the other moustached clones, Cynthia presumably, looked through the telescope and after a moment's fiddling with the control wheels gave a cheesy double thumbs-up. Fitch and the two Snooks gazed up at the Moon and wondered what exactly it had to do with the contraption's operation. Clearly feeling a little superfluous as the three identical weirdoes began to flick switches and turn dials, causing steam to cough from several brass orifices, one of the Snooks took out a tiny notebook and pencil and stood poised to record anything of interest. Nothing of any particular note took place however, apart from a rising hum, more puffs of steam and a slight glow of pearlescent light from the circular floor. Fitch, having braced himself for imminent death or transmogrification into a demon, or both, realised that not a lot had occurred and quite frankly the whole thing seemed to be a vast quantity of tedious mouth and not a great deal of splendidly tailored trousers. The two Snooks exchanged curious glances and then one of them, Wrenish perhaps, piped up,

'Are we waiting for anything in particular?' Ian looked up from his dials and replied brightly,

'Optimum operating temperature approaches.'

'Oh good,' replied Wrenish, or Rawlish, without really sounding like he meant it and made a little scribble with his slightly too small pencil in his undersized notebook. Rawlish, or Wrenish, for want of something better to do, glanced casually at his pocket watch.

Then apropos of entirely zipperoony Cynthia barked, 'EAR-MOO flight in final approach.'

Ian added cryptically whilst staring directly at the two Snooks 'Did you know that light is both a particle and a wave?'

Before Fitch or the Snooks could take in any of this crypto-babble the exotic material in the machine suddenly, but mercifully briefly, flared white hot, before relaxing to a shimmering glow. An innocuous but dense puff of smoke appeared between where Fitch was strapped to the gurney and the two Snooks stood looking less than impressed. However as the smoke cleared a small and distinctly curious figure could be seen standing in the centre of the circle with its back to Fitch, busying itself with what seemed to be a very large weapon of some description.

The figure was quite a thing, although hard to make out clearly, as it was clad in an extremely unusual looking red and gold spacesuit with a large tank of gas on its back and pipes feeding a green-tinged vapour into a large domed helmet. What little of its features that were visible within the helmet were very odd indeed. It was red-skinned and had a knotted little reptilian looking face with no nose, pointed ears, a wide spiky gold-toothed mouth and three eyes on stalks protruding from the top of its head. Curiously it was so preoccupied with trying to operate the large rifle type thing that it didn't seem to have noticed where it was or that anyone was looking at it. Eventually, and in a way that would have been comical if it hadn't been so darn weird, one of the three eyes looked up from the weapon and glanced with increasing alarm at its surroundings and the two Snooks gazing slack-jawed back at it. The other two eyes jolted upwards and stared intensely in three different directions.

'A demon, I presume? Jolly good,' muttered one of the Snooks. The other began scribbling in his tiny notebook once more.

However before further enquiries could be made, the newcomer panicked and flicked an operating switch on his giant plasma rifle. A great stream of hideous yellow light streaked from the weapon; narrowly missing the controls of the machine but neatly slicing Wrenish, or possibly Rawlish, clean in two. The sub-divided man's last words as the weapon continued to send bursts of fiendish light in all directions were probably 'Somewhat suboptimal,' before he gurgled his last. The little "Demon" barely three foot high, was clearly not in control of the fearsome light gun and in an effort to control it swivelled round and the edge of the beam caught Fitch's gurney sending him and it hurtling out of the machine and down into a rose bed with a mighty crash. Winded, but having survived much worse, Fitch realised that he'd fallen with his back and the full body of the trolley between him and the tooled-up imp. Instinctively he moved his arm to check for wounds and finding, with surprise, that it was now freed from the restraints moved with alacrity to unbuckle the remaining straps. Then without pause he rolled away from the rose bed and down the manicured lawns, before falling unceremoniously over what was, presumably, a previously unseen ha-ha. Behind him the sounds of plasma fire seemed to have died down and, grabbing a nearby rock - the only weapon to hand, Fitch peered cautiously over the stonework of the ha-ha to see if he was being pursued.

Looking back towards the great circular apparatus Fitch found, with great relief, that no one seemed to be pursuing him, presumably believing him dead or mortally wounded. The small creature had put down his over-sized weapon and was now standing at the machine's controls. Of the second Snook brother and Ian, Cynthia and co there was now no sign at all. Rather all the activity seemed to centre on the machine that was now popping with puffs of smoke and without any other sounds three more of the little demons appeared, this time accompanied by a three-legged sinuous robot and a large pile of bizarre pieces of equipment that vaguely resembled parts of the circular machine but on a much larger scale. As Fitch gazed on dumb-founded the tri-bot began to move the apparatus off the disc and the small creatures took up the controls where the moustachioed men had been earlier. Before he could make any further sense of it all, additional puffs of smoke and more equipment and tri-bots appeared. Again they moved rapidly to clear the items from the machine to allow even more to arrive. The pace seemed to be quickening all the time as the creatures and their machines carried out their fiendish plan. What Fitch needed now was an equally cunning plan, but nothing was yet suggesting itself. If these were indeed demons then they were extremely well equipped and much more organised than such spectres usually were. He glanced up at the moon again, now drifting past the vertical and waning to the west. Finally with a cold shudder he realised exactly what he was witnessing and knew that he had no option but to do something to stop it, or at the very least warn others.

'Demons, my arse,' he muttered to no one in particular.

As Fitch continued to observe more and more little creatures, tri-bots and other exotic contraptions continued to arrive. It was clear enough that they were obviously in a great hurry to construct another machine, several times larger than the first. Pieces were assembled by the tri-bots with great speed and skill. An even bigger tripod machine had arrived in a folded up state and after stretching out it's great jointed metal limbs had proceeded to demolish parts of a nearby town house to make more space for construction. The second giant disc-shaped apparatus was already nearing completion and Fitch could only imagine what giant monstrosities might arrive once it was functioning. His only slight hope was that the machines had some connection to the moon that meant that they could only operate whilst it was visible above. It was a very small hope to cling to, but all he had. Then, as he continued to observe, something else even more unusual caught his eye. As one of the great payloads arrived in another cloud of smoke, a small, four-legged creature wearing an oddly familiar, but very old-fashioned looking spacesuit complete with tiny helmet and oxygen tanks appeared from amongst the items and darted urgently for the cover of nearby mulberry bushes. Fitch had to blink and shake his head to make sure he had really seen it, but he was forced to conclude that he had. A cat in a spacesuit had just run from the machine and, if he wasn't dreaming, it bore Homeland Defence insignia.

'Oh for heaven's sake!' he growled to himself, but he realised that finding that cat was going have to be his priority now. There must be a clue in its sudden appearance, and judging by the way it moved, it knew not to hang around in the presence of these weird creatures.

Shifting his aching frame onto all fours Fitch began to crawl in an extremely undignified manner along the rough bricks of the ha-ha towards the mulberry bush where the cat had scampered for safety. Trying his best to keep a low profile, not easy for someone with Fitch's bulk, he dragged himself out of the ha-ha and into the shrubbery where he had last seen the be-suited feline. Sure enough as his eyes adjusted to the slight gloom in the bushes, he saw the cat sitting in its somewhat cumbersome spacesuit, clearly weary and scared, observing him wide-eyed with extreme anxiety. Fitch moved very slowly, partly so as not to not scare the animal and partly because he was in too much pain to do otherwise. The cat did indeed have on a very natty looking spacesuit, not a perfect fit but elegant enough in an old-fashioned sort of way. Just below his little helmet and breathing tube was, clearly enough, an enamelled badge that read "Homeland Defence" and a second one below that that read "Albion Expeditionary Force (Extraterrestrial)". More baffled by this than before Fitch edged closer, reaching out one muscular arm in what he intended to be a reassuring way, and for want of something more cat-friendly to say offered a grizzled, 'Here kitty, kitty', and added a hopeful, 'good kitty'.

The cat though, wasn't buying any of it, and just as Fitch inched close enough to make a lunge, it darted off with surprising speed leaving Fitch to fall into the dust. 'Bloody moggy,' he muttered, but had no real choice other than to follow it out of the bushes and into the large house in whose gardens they had been having such japes. Glancing over his shoulder as he crossed the threshold, Fitch observed anxiously that the creatures had nearly completed their second great circular machine and were already constructing a third. Two menacing great tripods stood towering over everything and the little armoured "demons" were running here and there setting up a variety of ugly looking weapons. Any thoughts of trying to stop them had long since left his head, all he wanted to do was get the blasted space cat and vamoose as quickly as he could.

Cautiously making his way into the drawing room onto which the door led, Fitch surmised that the house had probably once been owned by some sort of inventor, since most of the room was full of eccentric-looking items, the uses of which Fitch could not begin to imagine. He had no time to consider it further as he had a cat to find, and in a vain attempt to expedite this offered up another pathetic 'Here kitty-kitty.'

No felines being immediately visible, Fitch moved out of the drawing room and into a hallway, where with a slight start he noticed a small boy sitting at the bottom of an elegant staircase with, in his arms, the now entirely exhausted looking cat. Both looked at him with extremely wide, anxious eyes but made no attempt to run. It appeared they had clearly identified each other as similarly lost souls in a world gone decidedly mad. Fitch realised he was still carrying a rock and in his battered black leather trenchcoat probably looked about as scary as anything that was arriving outside. Moving very slowly so as to not startle them, Fitch placed the rock on a nearby occasional table and spread his arms slightly.

'I'm not going to hurt you, okay? I think we are all on the same side here. Do you speak English?' he asked the boy, who nodded without saying anything. 'Okay, good, my name is Fitch what's yours?'

'Tom,' replied the boy very quietly his mouth clearly very dry.

'Good lad Tom, now I'm guessing we are in Albion, perhaps even the Metropolis itself, am I right?' The boy nodded again and, somewhat curiously held out a hard-backed children's book towards Fitch with his free hand. The cat meanwhile had closed its eyes and seemed uninterested in taking any further part in proceedings. 'What's this?' growled Fitch, trying to restrain himself as best he could since he didn't really have time for picture books. However something about the child's insistence made him curious, and as he took the book he felt a shiver go down his spine. The tome was indeed a child's storybook of some sort, and on the cover embossed in gold letters were the chilling words "The Great Martian War". Fitch felt his hands tremble a little as he took this in.

'Page eight,' whispered the child and with slightly shaking hands Fitch opened the leaves and fumbled to find the page in question. When it finally fell open on the requisite page he saw a double spread illustration that was almost certainly meant to be the surface of some stark planet. On the left were a number of Albion commandos in armoured space suits, laser rifles in gloved hands, and on the right a towering tripod that was their adversary. The title of the page read: "Albion Commandos storm the Martian's moon base" but most tellingly of all, at the feet of the commandos, in identical four-limbed spacesuits to the one sitting on the boy's lap before him, were a number of cats. The rather prosaic caption beneath the animals read "Holomatron detecting cats" which left him none the wiser. His hands were still trembling somewhat at the magnitude of what the book was telling him and this caused one of the pages to flick over revealing an illustration that looked incredibly similar to the "demons" busy constructing bizarre installations outside. The suit was somewhat more old-fashioned looking, but the three eyes and glinting grin were unmistakable. The caption on this drawing read simply "Martian Soldier".

A crashing noise from behind him caused Fitch to spin on his heels and he found himself staring at one of the three-eyed aliens from the book, this one very much real and chuntering to itself in some weird language, a mean-looking plasma rifle pointing straight at them. Seconds after it had started talking a little grille a the bottom of its helmet sparked into life uttering in an artificial sounding, but oddly camp, metallic voice, 'Earth-grubbers surrender immediately!' Instead of obeying this Fitch slowly reversed the book to show it the picture,

'I know what you are,' he hissed. But, before he could elaborate more, the cat, which had revived itself somewhat, leapt at the alien, who swivelled two of its three eyes and gave a little shriek. Falling backwards it fired the gothic looking weapon and its sickly yellow beam sliced through the ceiling and sent a cascade of plaster and dust tumbling around them. 'Uh oh!' translated the metallic voice somewhat belatedly.

Finally in his element, Fitch moved quickly, grabbing the plasma rifle and slamming the butt into the alien's helmet sending a crack spidering through the glass dome. Wisps of sulphurous green smoke seeped out from the fractured helmet. The alien gave a gurgling little moan, which the grille translated shortly afterwards in entirely unsuitable sly tones as 'Help, mummy'.

'Too late for any of that Martian!' growled Fitch fumbling with the rifle until he eventually found the right controls and blasted the Martian, and most of the floor, in a stream of molten plasma fire. Evil-smelling smoke filled the room and, fearing further aliens arriving at any time, Fitch slung the rifle and moved to grab the boy and the now motionless-again cat. 'We are done here boy, do you know where there are any cars or carriages?' Coughing and shielding his mouth from the acrid smoke Tom nodded and began to lead them to an oak-panelled side door. Fitch strode after him; cat tucked under his arm, noting as he went that there was a message canister on the side of the cat's suit. He could only pray that it contained information that might help to improve the plight of humankind. With his free hand he unlatched the cat's space helmet and cast it to one side. The cat breathed what Fitch did not realise was its first ever mouthful of earth's atmosphere and trying his best to be gentle Fitch rubbed it between its ears.

'Whoever you are, you've done well. I'll get your message to those that will know what to do with it.' He hoped this was reassuring for the animal that seemed tired and heavy in his arms, but Fitch was not sure if even he believed his own words.

By turns they came to a garage and Fitch found a fuelled car and drove them all out onto the strangely deserted streets and away from the swelling ranks of the Martian war machine. His only plan was to leave the city; he now recognised as the Albion capital – Metropolis and attempt to reach the Prime Minister's country house that was not far away at Chartingfold Levels. Surely someone there could alert the necessary forces to the invasion now taking place in the heart of the capital. As he drove he glanced up and realised he was heading straight towards the now waning moon. Perhaps it was a trick of the light, but he could swear that it looked like the orange half-globe was letting off small streams of smoke. Now he knew they were in all kinds of unholy trouble. What other conclusion could one arrive at when it was clear, to all who had eyes to see, that the moon was on fire?

IX

In The Shadow Of The Moon – Part 3

All was not well at *Chartingfold Levels*, the PM's sprawling country residence. In fact, it could easily be said that all was decidedly under the weather, if not downright queasy. The PM himself had been on edge since the evacuation of the great capital city, the outline of which was just visible on the horizon from where the PM now stood anxiously fiddling with his pocket watch by the big drawing room bay window. Behind him staff with reports came and went and his private secretary Dr. Hieronymus Gunquit, stiffly formal in old-fashioned frock coat and breeches, did his best to shield him from the more outlandish rumours sweeping the government ranks like an outbreak of cattle plague. All in all, however, the increasingly troublesome briefings from the few scout patrols that had ventured into the suburbs in the last day or so, had at least completely vindicated their hasty decision to abandon the city. If there were any hope of normality being restored any time soon, it would be news to the PM. Gazing with a loose focus into the middle distance the PM slowly became aware of his scrupulously dignified secretary attempting to get his attention with a polite cough.

'Oh Gunquit, what is it now?' moaned the PM, who feared his heart might not be able to take any more bizarre happenings. 'Please no more bad news, for a hour or two at least.'

'Yes indeed Prime Minister, perhaps a glimmer of hope is twinkling on the horizon.' The PM spun around at this and saw that the twice-bespectacled (one pair for distance on his head, the reading frames clipped to his regal nose) grey-haired functionary was gripping a telegraph flimsy in each hand. 'But also portents of something deeply ominous,' he intoned.   Then on seeing the PM's distinctly crestfallen little face, added a kindly 'could be nothing of course'. The PM drew breath and readied himself for the absolute worst.

'Very well, break it to me gently Gunquit if you'd be so kind.'

'Naturally Prime Minister, naturally,' muttered the secretary glancing quickly between the two messages wondering which one to offer first. In the end he decided to save the better news until last.

'So, the Astronomer Royal is here, she seems a bit concerned about something.'

'That mad woman, I'm sure it's another of her hare-brained schemes,' chuckled the PM, glad that so far the news didn't seem too onerous.

'Quite, quite,' reassured Gunquit, 'I'm sure it's absolutely nothing, but apparently the moon is on fire.'

'The which is what?' exclaimed the PM, very much hoping he'd heard wrong.

'The moon, smoke and so forth, could be on fire, etcetera, etcetera. Almost certainly nothing,' countered Gunquit looking to try and change the subject as the PM seemed like he might be on the verge of a nervous breakdown.   'In other news,' he continued determinedly, 'The Lushthorpe's son has been found.' The PM was slightly struggling for breath at this point, but this was at least some more positive news,

'Tom-ish' he gurgled, almost correctly.

'Thomas, that's quite right Prime Minister,' acknowledged Gunquit with an only slightly condescending tone. 'One of our mercenary chaps has found him apparently, Titch or Bitch or somebody,' he added struggling to read the telegraph slip.

'Well finally a glimmer of good news,' breathed the PM, beginning to recover his usual ruddy disposition; all thoughts of rogue moon fires now temporarily forgotten. 'Have the Lushthorpes been informed?'

'Most assuredly prime minister,' cooed Gunquit relieved that the PM seemed suitably recovered. 'The rescue party are nearly here and Grenville and Griselda are on hand to receive him.'

At this point a slight rumpus in the corridor outside the drawing room caught both their attentions. 'Ah,' noted Gunquit, 'it would seem that Ms. Carshalton the Astronomer Royal is here. I'll be running along then.' The PM felt his heart sink as the distinctive tones of Ms. Scarlett Carshalton the eccentric planetologist and astronomer could indeed be heard talking boisterously outside.

'Oh there was one more thing,' added Gunquit with half his body already out of the door, 'apparently there is also a space-cat with a secret message.' And with this he attempted to exit the other half of his lithe frame and make good his escape, however the PM was close to apoplexy by this point.

'STAY GUNQUIT!' he roared and, with a sheepish glance and extreme reluctance the private secretary slunk back into the room. Before he could add further explanation though all talk of extra-terrestrial felines was halted by the unceremonious arrival of the king's astronomer in the very shape of Ms Scarlett Carshalton. Ms Carshalton was a beyond eccentric character clad today in vivid purple jacket, red breeches and non-matching shoes. Her hair was a spiky mass of blonde and red, her uneven angular features were somewhat interrupted by a clunky brass eyepiece clamped over a single eye, which was perhaps designed to be used with a modern telescope or something.

'Tuesday greetings to you my lord,' she began rather oddly, since it was quite clearly Wednesday. 'I don't want to inflate my own trumpet, but I have a dramatic denouncement,' she continued melodramatically.

'Is the moon on fire?' sighed the PM.

'The moon is…' her voice tailed off, 'Well how the love a chicken did you know?'

'You sent a message ahead,' interjected Gunquit proffering the telegraph slip.

'Lies!' declared Carshalton, acting as though her very integrity had been questioned. At this point the PM felt it necessary to step in before a fight ensued.

'Now, now Ms Carshalton, I'm sure there is a reasonable explanation for all this,' assured the PM, looking to calm everybody down a little before his own blood pressure hit the roof.

'I doubt it,' blurted the astronomer. 'The flamin' Moon is well, flaming!' she declared, and without invitation bellowed for two laboratory coat clad assistants to scuttle in and begin setting up a preposterously over-elaborate telescope in the bay window. At this point Gunquit wondered whether it might be prudent call the PM's physician since the leader seemed to have gone rather pale again, but in the end he had a better idea. Smartly pulling out a chair to take the PM's wobbling frame he also called for an orderly to come from the corridor.

'I'll get some tea, Prime Minister,' he purred in what he believed was a comforting sotto voce. 'And I'll get Mrs H-F to pop by. I'm sure she can clear all this up.' Carshalton declared this to be just the lickerty-ticket and the PM gratefully sank into the chair to recover his demeanour whilst Gunquit made the necessary arrangements.

Mrs Hildabrand-Fogg was the oldest serving member of the civil service and her vast knowledge and many, many years of advice to countless governments of all leanings and none made her counsel indispensible at moments of great crisis. Her near legendary memory meant that, despite many modern mechanical recalling-engines now being available, if you wanted to know something she was always the best place to start.

'Better get Coward and Buttercock too,' muttered the PM absentmindedly, feeling sure the Homeland Defence (and Attack) Secretary and Minister of Procurement would be required to do something even if it was just to make him feel slightly better. For the first time in about ten minutes, the PM felt it was actually safe to take a breath.

Disappointingly, for the PM at least, this idyllic moment lasted all of one half second before the doors were once more flung open and a quite monstrous figure in a battered black leather trenchcoat filled the oak-framed doorway. As if this sight was not startling enough, the figure was holding in his bulky arms a rather fluffy looking tabby cat (now mercifully relieved of it's antique spacesuit) that was looking on with an air of tired insouciance. The PM sprang to his feet and took a step forward,

'Titch I presume?' he enquired optimistically.

'Titch my mother's belly button!' chortled Carshalton who now had her eyepiece clamped onto the baroque telescope meaning that the whole tubular mechanism had to move with her, nearly knocking the head off one of her assistants, as she rotated to take a gander.

'Fitch,' snapped Fitch, 'Tobias Fitch, I have a message for you.'

'Quite, quite,' replied the PM trying to sound unflustered, 'from our friendly space cat who is...' he looked at his private secretary for assistance.

'Mrs Tickle the third,' growled Fitch, without a hint of levity and no one, not even the barmy astronomer, dared offer even a mild chortle. 'It's marked for the Prime Minister's eyes only'

'Oh, right,' gulped the PM, 'better let me see it then.' With that Gunquit moved with graceful elegance to accept the message tube, but it seemed, with growls from both Fitch and Mrs Tickle that they would only hand it over to the PM himself. Reluctantly he stepped aside and the PM, taking a deep breath to steady himself and, summoning his slender reserves of statesmanship, moved forward to take the message tube. The lid was wax-sealed and somewhat stiff, but after only a minute-or-so's struggling the PM did eventually manage to prise it open and pulled out the paper coiled up inside. He stared at it perplexed for what seemed like an age, before finally looking up to announce:

'It's in some sort of code, I can't make head nor tail of it.' Gunquit stepped forward to give his tuppence worth and, when he'd finally selected the right pair of spectacles, found that there was a solution to the conundrum.

'It's upside down prime minister,' he whispered not quite subtly enough for no one to notice.

'Ha, he's a right old nincompfish,' guffawed Carshalton from behind her telescope eye appendage. The PM went a shade of puce, and coughed to cover his embarrassment as he turned the piece of paper round and proceeded, after a slight pause and cough to clear his throat, to read aloud.

'The Foe returned stop, EAR-MOO B viable stop send help soonest if not sooner stop plus parts for MOO-EAR stop will hold out as long as possible stop God Save the Queen stop.' He shook his head disconsolately, 'Well it's total gibberish, for starters we've a king now, have done for nigh on ten years.' He passed the note to Gunquit for a second opinion, although he was quite sure there was nothing more that could be added. 'No no, this won't do at all, you're going to have to explain yourself Tickle!' he stared at Mrs Tickle III with what he thought was a withering prime-ministerial glare, but the cat gave him such a dirty look in return that he felt himself reddening again and was forced to look away. 'Where is Mrs H-F to make some sense of this ear-mooing nonsense?' he spluttered.

'What goes oom oom?' interjected Ms Carshalton without being asked, but before anyone could consider this further she continued, 'a cow going backwards,' and proceeded to laugh herself half to death.

'I'm here Horace,' announced the wizened tones of Mrs Hildabrand-Fogg as her immense frame waddled past Fitch and towards the PM. Mrs H-F was a rotund, but extremely ancient woman, whose creased face recounted the decades of valiant service she had given to the homeland. Her silver hair tied in the neatest of regulation buns; she walked steadily, but slowly with only a gnarled walnut cane for assistance. Pausing only to tickle Mrs Tickle between the ears and offer a cryptic, 'you're the spit of your great grandmother.' The cat purred contentedly with only a slightly melancholic after note.

'There's not time for any of that Gladys!' spluttered the PM who seemed to suddenly be on first name terms with the senior civil servant. 'Apparently this cat is from space, the moon is on fire and there's some sort of ear-mooing somewhere we need to fix yesterday, if not before. Really I don't know what to make of any of it! What's to be done?' Undeterred by any of this ranting, Mrs H-F tottered forwards and took the message from Gunquit, examined it carefully on both sides and then tutted to herself.

'Well we do have some chaps on the moon, why not ask them?'

'WHAT?!' exclaimed the PM in a quite unusual high-pitched squeaky tone and went bright red in the face. 'How the devil did I not know this?!' He glared at Gunquit and the astronomer in turn, who both shrugged and tried to look at something else. This was particularly tricky for Carshalton strapped to the telescope as she was and another head was nearly removed. 'Chaps on the moon and bloody moggies too no doubt!' yelled the PM who then felt his legs go slightly wobbly and Gunquit had to move sharply to prevent him collapsing. 'Get off me, I'm perfectly alright!' shouted the PM, although he clearly wasn't. 'Blasted chaps on the bally moon for heaven's sake, someone could have told me this, I'm only the bloody prime minister after all!'

'Oh I expect none of them knew, it was a while back now,' explained Mrs H-F, hoping this might calm things down a little, but if anything it seemed to make matters worse.

'Oh that's just ruddy perfect!' spluttered the PM. 'Incompetent bunch of buffoons the whole blasted bunch of them.'

At this point, before the PM could spontaneously combust the door opened yet again and the familiar shapes of The Right Honourable Arthur Coward - Homeland Defence (and Attack) Secretary - and Wrigley Buttercock (Procurement Minister) stepped in.

'Are we interrupting something?' enquired Coward politely, surveying the PM's murderous glare and the rest of the motley crew trying to avoid it. But before anyone could utter anything by way of reply the second figure, Buttercock, a rather handsomely moustachioed man with dark curly hair and a smart velvet jacket caused rather more of a commotion than a procurement minister had any right to evoke. As soon as he entered the room, Fitch had locked eyes with the familiar unblinking man. For a moment there was a staring standoff of South American proportions as neither man moved and then with a guttural yell of 'He's one of them!' Fitch had moved rapidly for a pistol hidden in his heavy coat. Before he could reach it however, Mrs Tickle beat him to the draw. With a screaming meow she leapt for Buttercock's feet and in less than an eye-blink the elegant man vanished. Leaving only the cat with something very small in its mouth and Fitch, pistol in hand, frantically scanning the room for his moustachioed nemesis. In this split second the PM's legs had finally given way and he'd passed out cold, meanwhile Ms Carshalton's hair appeared to have stood even further on end, should such a thing be possible. Once the commotion had died down a little, Mrs H-F bent over very slowly to pick up the cat and examine the small metallic object in her mouth, which resembled a tiny metal mouse on wheels. 'Good kitty,' she purred, 'good work, you've done your great grandmother very proud'.

Calling quickly for orderlies to attend the PM, and marines to secure the room, Gunquit turned to the senior civil servant and murmured, 'I think an explanation will be in order.'

Mrs H-F nodded sagely and, despite her great age and creaking bones, helped Gunquit attend the PM adding softy, 'I think what you young whippersnappers need is a history lesson.' And whether they liked it or not, that was what they were going to get.

Once order had been restored, the whole team, minus the long disappeared Buttercock, had moved under armed guard to the cabinet room, which was deemed to be more secure. Professor Lushthorpe was summoned to lend his technical advice, and the royal astronomer was reluctantly persuaded to unattached herself from her telescope contraption to attend unencumbered. Once all were assembled and tea and biccies finally served, Mrs H-F began to fill in the, still rather cross, PM and his staff on how it was that New Albion, or in matter of fact Olde Albion, came to have a force of some thirty or so soldiers stationed on the moon. It came out in this lecture that the whole force had been beamed there on one of these EAR-MOO, or if you prefer EARth to MOOn, light elevator contraptions some fifty-odd years previous, in order to counter the first Martian invasion of Earth. They were, as had been alluded to, cats amongst their company who's primary job was to detect Martian holomatrons, or hard light people. With Fitch also contributing his recent adventures, it became apparent that these light people had already infiltrated the government at the very highest levels and had been directing operatives to retrieve parts for the light elevators from all corners of the globe; seemingly at the behest of the government, but all along it had been to construct an elevator receiver station to commence a new invasion of Earth. Why they had returned and how they were to be defeated were beyond the understanding of Mrs H-F despite her razor sharp memories of the first Great Martian War, but she vowed to work with all concerned to get answers to these questions.

Although the knowledge for training holomatron-detecting cats (along with an entire moonbase full of commandos) had long been lost from collective memory, it seemed that they had managed somehow to keep the training alive on the moon, and they thanked all that was holy that Mrs Tickle III was now here to sweep the halls of government clear and assist in training a new generation of cats. Fitch, with his close encounter with new arrivals and stolen plasma gun, was tasked with assisting with defence, and help with planning an immediate offensive to attempt to disable the new MOO-EAR before more war materiel could be transported down.

In a final decision it was resolved to try and work out where in the world the fabled EAR-MOO B might be located, and if there was anything at all that could be done to get it working again. Then perhaps, they could send more troops to the moon and get to the bottom of what was going on up there, and how and why it came to be on fire. It was with a grim determination and a sober realisation that the PM called the cabinet meeting to a close, shaken to his very core by the knowledge that the second Great Martian War was now upon them.

X

In The Shadow Of The Moon – Part 1

Every morning private (first class) Erasmus Trout started his day the same way: enjoying a bitter-tasting tumbler of Cookie's best earthshine in the back of the cobbled together field kitchen unit, before helping Cookie making breakfast for the troop. It was a ritual in which he had indulged so many times that he had completely lost count. Cookie's company though was always a pleasure, it had once been said that the rotund, ruddy-faced chef was the man who put the gin in original, but again Trout's fading memory did not supply the name of the wit who had coined this. Quite what was in Cookie's earthshine was a question that the wiry, long limbed Trout chose not to dwell on for too long. After all, there were only three sources of food in their sprawling bunker complex, hydroponically grown vegetables, a dwindling resource of preserved goods and waste products from the former two. No, best not to consider it too hard, indeed best not to consider the whole situation in too much depth lest one lose what little was left of one's sanity. No, far better to simply enjoy the tranquil moment of a pre-breakfast snorter with a chum and then lose oneself in the military regime that had been his lot for his entire adult life. In fact he often considered at this quiet time of reflection that he was, on the whole, pretty content with his status as a lifer, a career soldier for the duration, a warrior for all seasons, not that they saw many of those in this posting. The routine and discipline suited him to a tee. Had his life panned out differently, he was quite sure he would have stayed in the army anyway for long as he could. Mind you, in that scenario he would have been retired now for six years, for in just three weeks he would turn seventy-one. This thought was interrupted by the mewing entrance of his favourite feline, the wonderfully sleek Princess Azalea, looking for a pre-breakfast treat of her own. Cookie shrugged as he prepared to peel vegetables, he had nothing much to offer. In consolation Trout eased his arthritic bones off the stool and topped up the cat's water bowl from an ornate brass tap.

'There you go girl, breakfast is on its way,' murmured Trout to the cat. She shot him a look that was distinctly unimpressed but lapped up a little anyway. The water here tasted pretty odd, mused Trout to himself, but one got used to it. In truth it was all the Princess had ever tasted anyway, so she knew no different.

'Those blessed spuds won't peel themselves Trout,' admonished Cookie in his thick accent, with only a little annoyance creeping into his voice, as he downed the last of his stiffener and started to busy his well proportioned frame with the preparations.

'Right-oh cookie,' replied Trout doing likewise and grabbing a homemade apron to protect his venerable, oft-repaired uniform. 'Let's get this rocket on the launchpad once more.'

After a meagre breakfast the whole platoon, thirty men, and (slightly more) accompanying cats, shuffled their way into the drill hall for the next part of their morning ritual.

'Come along now gentlemen, pick it up a bit,' barked Sergeant Roger 'Wilco' Rogers in his annoyingly brusque manner.

'Oh give it a rest Wilco,' muttered corporal Ezra Longstocking, the oldest and most white-haired of their company, as he eased himself into line and straightened down his tatty Homeland Defence uniform jacket. 'We're all hobbling as fast as we can,' he added, with a wink.

'Less of your lip, me young fella-me-lad!' snapped Sergeant Rogers, with no obvious hint of irony.

'Less of your young!' chortled Longstocking by way of reply, since he was seventy-three years old if he was a day, 'A little respect for the elderly if you please.' Private Algie "Chatty" Chattenborough, who was indeed the youngest of their company at a spritely sixty-seven years and a hundred and forty six days, said nothing. Before Rogers could think of something militarily significant, yet witty, to counter with, he was obliged to utter,

'Troop! Troop atten-shun!' as captain Humpty Willingsmouth blustered into the room a beaming smile all over his ruddy moustachioed face.

'What, what, what, what, what?' intoned the Captain jovially as he moved up to inspect his motley troop. 'What's all this complaining?' He placed himself front and centre and folded one hand behind his back whilst with the other he straightened the ends of his, really rather exquisite, handlebar moustache. The assembled troopers all sighed quite audibly at this, since it was a clear sign that captain Humpty was about to deliver one of his trademark lectures.

'Quiet!' bellowed sergeant Rogers.

'Roger roger wilco,' chortled Longstocking under his breath, a joke that, unlike the assembled platoon, showed no sign of getting old.

More guffaws were cut short as Rogers rounded on the unfortunate corporal.

'Now look 'ere Longstocking, you're not too old to be thrown in the brig y'know.'

'Oh yeah, by you and who's stairlift?'

'Now then men, settle down,' interjected their captain, with only the slightest note of impatience. 'I'm not going to stand for any of this *old* talk. It's a well known fact that you are only as old as the woman you feel.'

'What women would these be?' muttered someone from the second row with note of melancholy tingeing his tone. If the captain had heard, he chose not to show it.

'Now I don't know if you are aware of it, but this coming Tuesday will be our fiftieth anniversary of taking Fortress Gwendolyn.' A murmur of some surprise went around the assembled men. 'And I for one don't feel in the slightest bit different to when I led you all to this great victory. No indeed, I can safely say without the slightest fear of contradiction that I have never felt finer in all of my life. Furthermore...' captain Humpty stopped at this point and a rather odd expression came onto his face, which seemed to have lost a little of its rosy complexion. He looked as if he was going to say something else, but the only sound that came out was a slightly croaky gurgle, and with this he promptly collapsed with all the grace of a felled oak gently falling to the earth. For a second or two there was stunned silence, as no one was quite sure whether this was some sort of jape from the jovial captain or a real emergency. Finally after what seemed an age in which the captain did not move a muscle, private Godwin Purpletree remembered that he was indeed the designated first aider and moved in a rather less than spritely manner to attend the fallen officer. Ignoring the plaintive mutterings of 'I haven't dismissed you yet,' from Rogers, the other soldiers pushed past him to form a loose group around the body. Purpletree felt for a pulse and then looked up, his face quite ashen.

'He's gone,' was all he could find to say, before tugging his cap from his head and clutching it to his chest. The others started to do the same and an odd sniffle was heard being stifled. It was quite astonishing, to those who cared to dwell on it, that in all their near fifty years in the fortress this was the first soul they had lost, to combat or otherwise. That it should be their commander-in-chief made it all the more poignant.

'What do we do now?' enquired Trout, somewhat forlornly, and since no one really knew, nothing was offered by way of response. Indeed, such was the lack of precedent to the unfortunate event, that the septuagenarians might well have stood dumb-mouthed for quite some minutes more, had their reverie not been interrupted by the sudden arrival in the parade hall of six or so additional cats in a state of some excitement. Leading this pack was Princess Azalea, who made straight for private Trout and rubbed herself on his leg to get his attention.

'Not now princess,' mumbled Trout, wiping the hint of another tear from his phlegmy eyes. But as he glanced down at the cat, who was still arching her back against his calf, he couldn't help but notice that she had something in her mouth; a strange, metallic object that seemed to be buzzing, or alive in some way. 'What on Jupiter?' muttered Trout as he reached down to take the object from the animal, who was clearly very pleased with herself. Once he had it in his hand, a chill went through him as he recognised it immediately, despite the fact that the last time he'd seen one was nearly fifty years previously. It was a small metal device in roughly the shape of a mouse with four large rubber wheels, which now spinning furiously as it tried to get away. 'Holomatron!' he exclaimed, before quickly placing it on the floor on its back, so it could not make good its escape, and put it out of its misery with the heel of his size eight boots, sending metal fragments in all directions. 'Now where in the world did you get that from?' he asked the cat urgently. In response, Princess Azalea mewed loudly and headed out of the room, the other cats hot on her paws. It seemed that someone was going to have to take charge of the situation, and since Trout was the only one who didn't appear to be lost in his thoughts, it seemed to come down to him.

'Sergeant, you're our leader now, get the captain somewhere safe. Ezra, Algie with me, let's see what the cats have found.' With these words the men seemed to snap out of their idyll and the years of military discipline began to reassert themselves. Trout and his two chums strode with purpose in pursuit of the cats one of which, who went by the moniker Marvin Moonunit, had waited at the corner of the drill hall airlock until they hobbled to catch him up. Adrenaline was beginning to course through his veins and Trout found that with each step his stiffness seemed to ease a little and he soon found himself loping along the corridors at a fair old lickerty-split.

Fortress Gwendolyn, named for the Queen of Albion naturally, was quite a place since the vast majority of it had not been built by humans. Colossal domes filled with various gases - hydrogen, oxygen and nitrogen being the principle ones - made up most of it. Connecting this were a series of corridors and bunkers, many of which the soldiers had enlarged, or repurposed for a variety of uses. Even now they moved rapidly past sleeping quarters, storerooms, and various arcane machines chuntering away on the vital services that kept them all in the land of the living. Ahead of them, the cats waited at every corner for the lumbering humans to reach them and then sprinted on again. Eventually they reached their intended destination, which was a particularly militarised bunker that appeared to be part observatory, part weather station with shuttered, heavily glazed window slits pointing to all points of the compass. The walls were adorned with a huge variety of brass dials and near the windows stood a myriad of baroque telescopes, binoculars and, indeed, trinoculars of both human and alien origin. The cats all moved to one particular set of looking glasses that were aligned to a shuttered window on the far side of the room, seemingly urging the accompanying men to take a look. The cats that dwelt with the soldiers in Fortress Gwendolyn had been specially bred to detect aliens and their holomatrons, and even these ones, three generations on from the original inhabitants of the bunker, retained these unearthly skills. Of course there are some that say that cats were brought to earth originally by extra-terrestrials, but this has never been proved one way or another to anyone's particular satisfaction. Nevertheless, these particular felines have always seemed very switched on when it came to military matters. Following their lead, Trout and Chattenborough moved to force open the great iron shutters on the bunker viewing port, whilst Longstocking (as the more senior man) swung the highly complicated looking glasses into position to see out. With slightly trembling bony fingers he moved to the eyepieces and fiddled with the focussing mechanism. Before long he let out a short gasp.

'What is it, what can you see?' enquired Trout, feeling his anxiety rising steadily.

'Better take a look for yourself and make sure an old man hasn't just hallucinated it,' replied the corporal, backing away from the eyepieces so Trout could position himself to take a look. Blinking hard as he moved the wheel to focus the binoculars private Trout started to take in what he could see. For many miles ahead the whole cratered landscape came into focus, and at first he was not sure what he was supposed to be seeing. Then with a start he saw them, silhouetted on the very far horizon, a whole series of circles, barely visible at the maximum magnification of the viewing apparatus.

'Martian war wheels,' he breathed, hardly able to believe what he was seeing. He defocussed and refocused the machine again, just to make sure, but there was no mistake. He could clearly see the gigantic circular structures of three or four enormous Martian war wheels, evidently in the final stages of being constructed. Looking further, there were clearly other machines, robots and rockets all visible, and beyond that the great blue and white circle of the Earth hung ominously in the pitch-black sky. There could be no doubting it. Fifty years, almost to the day, the previously vanquished Martian marauders had returned to the Moon.

Leaving Algie "Chatty" Chattenborough, who still had not uttered a word, in the observation post with orders to telegraph through any changes in the demeanour of the invaders, Trout and Longstocking hot-booted it back to the drill hall. On arrival they were heartened to find that corpse of poor old captain Humpty Willingsmouth had been removed to one of Cookie's empty freezers. The news of the Martian re-invasion was met with sober silence and then a degree of military efficiency as the troopers began to put their plans together. It was soon clear from initial discussions that, despite all his bluster, sergeant Rogers was unlikely to be of much use as a war leader and the soldiers were increasingly looking to Longstocking for direction.

'We need lookouts posting at all four observatories, to report on the hour every hour, unless there is a major incursion of forces,' began the corporal. Nods all round before troopers were despatched to begin their watches. 'Double patrols from our feline friends also, in case of further holomatron appearances.' This was directed towards the cats lurking amongst the legs of the troopers. It was met mainly with insouciance, but eventually one of the cats, a particularly mischievous fellow named simply Fluffy McFluffball, left to spread the word. Or whatever it was that cats did in such circumstances. The attendance in the drill hall started to thin out, and sergeant Rogers also slipped off, announcing that he needed to take a call of nature, but after he left is was agreed that they were better off without him.

'Cookie, Trout, Flashman – council of war in the kitchen I think,' ordered Longstocking and with that they retired to the field kitchen to see if any kind of strategy could be, ahem, cooked up.

As they bustled into the small unit and without waiting to be asked, Cookie cracked open a fresh bottle of hooch and poured them all a little over the usual two fingers.

'Hair of the frog,' muttered Cookie, without really making sense. The men took a welcome sip and then fell silent in consideration of their circumstances. Longstocking found his voice first,

'What direction did you see the enemy?'

'West, out beyond the hydrogen domes. What else is out that way?' replied Trout.

'The domes, and some of their old storage nonsense only...' offered private Inpan Flashman, a rather clever fellow of Asian descent, who knew that sector better than anyone, '...no wait, that's the location of MAR-MOO A. They must be aiming to repair it and bring more hordes from Mars!'

'Are we so old that we've managed to miss the arrival of a whole Martian army?' lamented Longstocking, clearly feeling very disappointed that this had happened on his watch.

'We've scouted and patrolled flawlessly for fifty years,' interjected Trout, looking to lift the mood, which had sunk to a notch or two below utterly despondent. 'They can only just have arrived, hence why the holomatrons have only just started to re-activate. We have to strike them now, before they can establish a foothold.'

'But what can we do?' wailed Flashman.

'Fight back,' confirmed Trout with steely resolution. 'Get a message to Earth if we can. They are sure to build a MOO-EAR on the Earth side, we have to get a message into one of their outbound flights,' Trout was almost beginning to convince himself, he just hoped the others were coming along with him. He swallowed another sharp mouthful of earthshine for a little lunar comfort.

'And fight we will,' confirmed Longstocking downing his tumbler and rising stiffly to his feet. 'I know how too, but it won't be a walk in the park. It will be strictly volunteers only. Break out the armoury, get everyone on a war footing and then assemble those not on guard duty back in the drill hall, there is not a moment to lose.' And with that the council of war was ended and the four old men rose stiffly to their duties.

Half an hour later, now suitably armed and fitted out in a motley array of ancient uniforms and creaking space suits. The thirty odd troopers, and three dozen cats, of the Homeland Defence - Albion Expeditionary Force (Extra-terrestrial) re-assembled in the drill hall in clusters of nervous conversation. Sergeant Rogers had reappeared, having presumably taken a long hard look at himself in the reflecting glass-o-scope, and seemed ready to resume some sort of executive control. However his only contribution turned out to be to simply mutter 'Carry on corporal' and then take a metaphorical, and indeed literal, step back from proceedings. Corporal Longstocking called the room to order and all eyes, human and feline turned to him in nervous anticipation.

'Now then men, you know I'm not one for speeches,' began Longstocking rather tentatively. 'So I'll get straight down to it. As you all know the old enemy has returned and they are already assembling their great war machines. There can be no doubt they intend to subdue the Moon and re-invade the Earth all over again.' No other sound could be heard now as Longstocking continued to address the ensemble. 'However the fiends have made a fundamental error by, presumably, believing our little force is of no consequence to them. How wrong they are! We will make them pay for their mistake and warn the earth of their arrival into the bargain. Make no mistake though, this will not be a bed of roses. It may not be possible for us to carry out my plan and also live on to see our hoped for victory. That is why I am asking for volunteers for these missions. Those who's hearts are made of stout oak and who can think only of the homeland and of glory.' He looked around the room at the men, several of whom had their eyes tightly closed in consideration of his words.

'Brave comrades, time is of the essence so I will ask all those men, and cats naturally, willing to put themselves in harm's way to take a step forward.'

Private Trout was one of those who's eyes were tightly shut, he had barely heard Longstocking's words since he had already been thinking over the agreed plan and realised that he had no choice; soldier that he was, borne only to know service. Without opening his eyes, he took what he believed was a firm and strong step forward. On opening his eyes though, he was mildly alarmed that perhaps his old mind had merely imagined him volunteering, as his place amongst the men hadn't changed; he was still in line. It was only after a moment's consideration, noticing the closer positioning of the corporal, that he realised that every single man and animal had moved forward as one. With this realisation he felt moisture welling in his eyes for the second time that day.

The plan, such as it was, was brutal in its simplicity. Four men and four cats were chosen from the ranks by drawing lots. Each pairing of human and feline had a mission, three of the couplings were to venture to the massive domes of hydrogen near to the Martian's new landings and with the aid of dynamite blow them to kingdom come, hopefully taking as many of the invaders with them as they could. The bonus of the plan was that it also denied the invaders a key resource and, should the second part of the plan fail, a big enough explosion that might be visible to warn those on the earth. The fourth pair would attempt to get close enough to see if a new MOO-EAR light transmitter had been built and if so, sneak the cat into the elevator with a message to rally support in the homeland.

Flashman and Trout had been detailed to compose the all-important message, but Flashman's first attempt had been deemed too alarmist, perhaps it was the five "HELPS!" (capital letters, exclamation mark) at the start that got it off on the wrong metaphorical foot. Trout's effort seemed to hit the right note:

"The Foe returned stop, EAR-MOO B viable stop. Send help soonest if not sooner stop. Plus parts for MOO-EAR stop. Will hold out as long as possible stop. God Save the Queen stop." The cat / man pairing selected for this task was "Chatty" Chattenborough and Mrs Tickle, a somewhat fluffy tabby cat generally thought of as a good egg, the third of her name to serve on the Moon. Chattenborough collected the message with only a simple nod and secured it in a wax-sealed message canister on the side of Mrs Tickle's cat-sized spacesuit. Without another word from Chatty, or indeed any at all, they were gone about their task, with only a few dry-mouthed *good lucks* and *godspeeds* to send them on their way. Of the three other pairings, it turned out that Erasmus Trout and Princess Azalea would be the last to get underway. The cat would normally be a bundle of energy, but in her small spacesuit with the dynamite and fuse attached securely with electrical tape, she suddenly seemed very quiet and demure. Trout hauled his complaining bones into his own armoured spacesuit and picking up the stoic feline, he said his goodbyes and had a long hug with Cookie before he fastened his helmet on and began his slow stomp down the old corridors of the moon base for, possibly, the last time.

When they had first arrived on the Moon, the Martians had evaded detection for a very long time, and had managed to build a great complex of tunnels, bunkers and gas storage domes. Quite what the exact purpose of these great hoards of hydrogen, oxygen and nitrogen were the humans never did discover. But they were grateful, not just for a nearly inexhaustible supply of breathable gases, but now it seems some ready-made bombs. Most of the Martian's tunnels were too small for humans and the cats were tasked with patrolling these, but fortunately the Martian's ever-present tri-bots were a little larger than humans and their service tunnels proved perfect for getting around the place. As he clomped along one of these over-engineered tunnels private Erasmus Trout had plenty of time to think since the journey to the nearest (and greatest) of the giant hydrogen domes was a good four mile trek. Princess Azalea was very quiet and still in his arms, he'd left her helmet off for now, in order to occasionally tickle her between the ears with a gauntleted hand, but there had been none of her usual purring in reply. Despite the imminent sacrifice that he and the cat were preparing to make, Trout could not help but feel a slight sense of elation. He was finally getting to be a warrior again, after forty-nine years of non-martial fannying around. Was this not after all the way for old soldiers to go, after decades of service, in a blaze of glory for the Homeland? He wondered if the cat understood this too, his instinct told him that she did. He went over the plan again in his head, it was simple enough that even his failing memory would have trouble forgetting it. His job was to deliver the Princess to the hydrogen dome, taking care of any Martians that might stand in his way, and deliver her and her explosive cargo into the service airlock. He glanced down at the fuse on the dynamite strapped to her back, it was about a three minute fuse. He might cut it down a bit, no sense in delaying the inevitable, he wasn't bothered about getting clear, he'd simply guard the door until the whole lot went up. He was ready to do it, although it did seem a waste in the way, it would be better if he could get far enough away to survive and fight on for a little longer. But under no circumstances would he allow Princess

Azalea to make the ultimate sacrifice if he wasn't prepared to make it too.

His mind was so lost in thought that the entrance to the great hydrogen dome came along much sooner than he had expected. With a gulp he put the Princess down and checked his rifle before venturing over to a small observation port that had views of the moonscape outside. The scene that confronted him was almost overwhelming. Martians in armoured suits and tri-bots were going this way and that, tapping into the great fuel domes and building exotic contraptions. Craning his neck to look up he could see the monumental arc of a giant war wheel being fuelled, it's chuntering engine already belching acrid steam into the vacuum.

He turned away, before the sight put him off his mission. He bent down to secure the small helmet onto his feline companion, and reached for a blade on his utility belt to shorten the fuse.

'Goodbye old girl,' he whispered hoarsely. The cat did not make eye contact with him so he busied himself checking the payload and the strap holding it to her back. As he prepared to shorten the wick a thought came rushing into his head that might mean it wasn't goodbye after all. Perhaps he could give the moggy a chance. Quickly as he could he put the knife down and reached for reinforced tape in a suit pannier. 'I've got an idea old girl,' this time the cat did look up, questioning what he was doing. Pulling off his gauntlets to make the job easier, he undid the strap holding the dynamite and instead taped the fuse across the gap with metal-backed tape. 'This is how it works old girl, the fuse will burn until it gets to the gap and then when it passes the tape the bomb will fall off. You'll have about a minute to get clear, so make it count.' And with that he replaced his gloves and ensured his helmet and oxygen tank were secure, before checking the cat's. Then without further words he lit the wick and lifted the cat up to the service airlock and popped her in; dynamite, fizzing fuse and all. Shutting the airlock, he activated the sequence to release her the other side and then moved to the intercom. As succinctly as he could he relayed what he had done in the hope that the other cats might benefit from the same modification to their payload. Then he was off, stomping back towards the base with his rifle in his hands.

As he walked the long three minutes before the fuse would reach the bomb, Trout found he was recalling long forgotten thoughts from his past, including his two score years on the planet earth before the moon became his home. Perhaps this is what they mean by your life flashing in front of your eyes, he mused. He recalled his morning tipple with Cookie and wondered if he'd live long enough to enjoy another glass with his dear friend. He thought of the other friends and comrades in his troop and how much they all meant to him. He chuckled at the thought of them all volunteering together and thinking that he'd just imagined it. It occurred to him with a feeling that could simply be thought of as happiness that he was entirely comfortable with his lot as a lifer, career soldier for the duration, warrior for all seasons.

'Who'd have thought?' he laughed out loud just to hear his voice.

At that exact moment there was a tremendous flash of blinding light and a second later a thundering shockwave knocked him clean off his feet and sent him crashing down and along the corridor. Finally a great roar of biblical proportions engulfed him and flames seemed to rush past him like great dragon's tongues. 'Good girl' he thought, 'good work Princess' and with that he lost consciousness.

When private Erasmus Trout came round some time later, he could only imagine he was in hell. All he could see was a thick black smoke and the odd lick of flame, he was in great pain and his ears were ringing. Gradually the view cleared enough to see that he was lying face up in the service corridor. His breath misting up the visor of his spacesuit, obscuring what little view he had, he gave out a chuckle, 'I'm bloody alive, you Martian bastards! There is fight in this old soldier yet!' He laughed again, louder this time and was just beginning to contemplate seeing if he could haul his old frame to its feet when something landed hard on his chest. He gasped desperately and tried to grope around for his rifle, but he couldn't feel it anywhere. 'Get off me you devil,' he yelled, but before he could take any further action a pair of wide, bloodshot, cat eyes starred down at him from inside a charred and blackened helmet and gave a plaintive, almost silent, meow. This time Trout found that he could not hold back his tears. He cried and cried and laughed and cried, until the tears stung his eyes.

The End (for now)

Printed in Poland
by Amazon Fulfillment
Poland Sp. z o.o., Wrocław

53331840R00106